This is a work of fiction. Any ı
and incidents are products of tł
fictitiously and are not to be co
actual events, locales, organiza
is entirely coincidental.

MW00967369

SAVAGE ANGEL copyright @ 2019 by Brook Wilder and
Scholae Palatina Inc. All rights reserved. No part of this book may
be used or reproduced in any manner whatsoever without written
permission except in the case of brief quotations embedded in
critical articles or reviews.

Follow Brook Wilder on Instagram at @authorbrookwilder!

TABLE OF CONTENTS

SAVAGE ANGEL
Chapter 1
Kristina

I took a slow, deep breath as I watched the caravan rumbling up the road through the scope of the gun, feeling the thrill of anticipation shoot through my body. While they were still a few miles out, I knew the time to attack was drawing close. After three hours of waiting for them to arrive, it was about to be on.

The dry desert heat had become quite annoying, and I longed for a good, cold beer to wet my parched lips. I'd have one once this was over and done with. Tonight, we would celebrate our victory and enjoy our pause before the war started that would no doubt come barreling our way after this fallout.

As the president of the Hell's Bitches bike club, it was my job to make the other club's day a bad one. I reveled in the fact that with each human trafficking shipment thwarted, some high-ranking member of that club was somewhere, throwing something and cursing my name and my club's.

I enjoyed bringing that kind of anger to a bunch of men. Actually, it was my life's goal.

And I was about to bring it to the one man I wished would drop off the face of the earth.

"You're thinking about him."

I turned to my second in command, arching a brow. "What?"

Mama Bear gave me a look, a spark of laughter in her pale blue eyes. Opal was her real name, though no one had the balls to call her that to her face lest they end up with a knife in their gut. She had knife skills I'd never seen before, and rumor was she learned from her daddy before they put him away in federal prison for killing a man.

We all knew her nickname was something she was quite proud of; Mama Bear was the only mom in the club; with two kids who were the apples of her eye. For that reason, I didn't like to take her on these missions.

She had something to live for. The rest of us, including me, didn't.

But right now, I hated the fact that she could read me like a book. "I'm not thinking about anyone," I said defiantly before turning back to the scope. "You need to get a hobby."

She laughed, her leathers scraping across the dirt and rocks as she got into a better position for the impending attack. "You're so full of shit, Kris. What you need is a pretty boy in your bed tonight. That will make you forget all about Rex."

My chest ached at the sound of his name, the same way it had for the last five years. I used to believe that old saying about time healing old wounds, but it didn't hold true with this wound. My pain did nothing but fester and I doubted I would ever get over the heartbreak. "My bed is always warm. Yours on the other hand…"

"Is cold as ice," she finished for me, a cackle escaping her. "Just the way I like it these days. I ain't got time to deal with a man. Those kids keep me busy enough."

"That and you would probably end up pregnant again," I teased, watching the caravan draw closer.

Mama Bear sighed. "You're probably right. Two's more than enough."

I refocused the scope, thinking about our banter. Mama Bear knew me better than anyone, having been there from the beginning. I'd started Hell's Bitches five years ago after Rex and I had our falling out. I was out to prove a club could be more than just a bunch of burly men riding on their bikes, breaking their women's hearts.

Okay, maybe only my heart had been broken.

But still, a woman could be just as tough as a man and I had proved it over and over again. My club was fifty strong, all women who could ride, shoot, and knife like the best of them. I personally interviewed and initiated my own prospects, never wanting to have someone who couldn't handle their shit trying to back me up in a fight.

I had some of the strongest women in Texas.

Seeing that the caravan was approaching the first pick point, I pulled my gun back and got to my feet. "It's time. Let's ride out."

There was a flurry of activity as I climbed onto my bike and slowly maneuvered it down the rocky outcropping we had been using as the lookout point. The hard leather seat burned me through my jeans. My bike was my baby, the only present I hadn't parted with since that day five years ago. I probably should have sold the damn thing; maybe that was the reason I couldn't put the past behind me, but I couldn't help myself.

I loved my bike. The seat was custom made, the paint scheme a swirl of greens, golds, and blues; all of my favorite colors. I honestly didn't even notice the small initials that were intertwined on the tank anymore, so small anyone else wouldn't notice it.

I knew they were there and what they had stood for.

Shaking out of the thought, I slid the bike behind a huge boulder with the rest of the women, grabbing my gun in the process. Heavily armed with this one, I wondered when the Pacific Cartel would double up on their security considering this was our fifth hit this month alone. Surprisingly, there were no Rough Jesters in attendance, which made me worry about an ambush. While we'd set up checkpoints all along the route and each one had come out clean, I still had this nagging sensation someone was out there, lurking in the shadows.

I held up my hand as the rumbling grew louder, noting the drone that followed the truck at a distance. What the hell was that thing for anyway?

Well, at least Rex would have a front seat to see me take down another one of the runs.

With a smile on my face, I pulled out my pistol from the waistband of my jeans and checked the rounds, ensuring nothing had changed from the last time I'd checked it.

This was the moment I craved, the one that brought me all kinds of feels. It was also the moment I thought Rex and I had shared together. I thought we had understood each other and connected on the same wave length.

Boy I had been wrong all the way around. Rex didn't want me on the same wave length as him. He had wanted me to be the pretty girl sitting on his lap or waiting in the wings for the 'men' to come back from handling business.

Well, I was about to show him yet again that he had been wrong on both accounts. I wasn't about to waste my skills over being some man's property. I wasn't just a pretty face.

I was the Widow Maker. "Let's do this."

The road exploded in front of the truck and it screeched to a halt, giving us enough time to surround it before they even knew what was going on. I wrenched open the door to the driver side, shooting the driver before he had a chance to pull his own gun, the bullet hitting him dead center between the eyes. Blood sprayed against the passenger window, but I didn't even bat an eye. "Cab's clear."

"Road's clear," Eileen 'Siren' Vaughn, called out, her voice floating in the breeze. She and some of the other women had scouted the checkpoints earlier. Siren was my road captain, though looking at her you wouldn't have expected her to be part of a women's bike club. The other women teased her endlessly about her dainty looks, but beneath the sweet and innocent face was a hellcat with claws to match.

I straightened my shoulders, holding my gun to my side. "Let's see what we have then." Cautiously, I approached the back of the truck, waiting for the moment men would pour out of the back and catch us off guard.

When it didn't happen, I yanked up the sliding door, surprised to see it packed full of crates, no doubt full of drugs and guns bound for Mexico. Another shipment I would sell to fund our cause and our club. I didn't feel any emotional attachment to the drugs or the guns, knowing I couldn't stop all the runs that left this place every single day.

So, I might as well make money off it.

It was the human trafficking I couldn't stand. The Pacifica Cartel was into stealing girls, women, and sometimes young boys for the evils of the world who were then sold into private prostitution or thrown onto the street to make money for the cartel.

I hated it. The one thing I hated more was that the Rough Jesters supported those runs.

Climbing into the truck, I moved to the back, drawing up short when I saw a person lying on her side amongst the boxes. "Shit," I said, crouching down to touch her shoulder. The back of the metal truck trapped the dry Texas heat inside making the temperature soar, and there was no telling how long she had been back here, suffering.

I gently turned her over, not at all surprised to see a beautiful young woman in front of me, her mouth taped shut and her arms tied behind her. Her eyes fluttered, then opened, and I tucked my gun back into my jeans, attempting to look non-threatening. "You're okay. I-we are rescuing you."

She blinked rapidly as I reached down and carefully removed the tape from her mouth before pulling out my knife to slice through the ropes tied at her wrists. She flinched, but I didn't stop sawing through them until they broke free.

"Can you stand?" I asked, sliding the knife back into the sheath strapped to my thigh.

"I, yes," she said, her voice cracking.

I grabbed her arm gently and helped her to her feet, steadying her as she wobbled a bit. "Come on, let's get you out of here."

The women moved aside, and I jumped down from the truck, then helped her down.

"Thank you," she said as someone passed her a bottle of water. "I'm Leigh."

"Kris," I said, wiping the sweat from my brow. "Sit on the bumper there and get your bearings. We'll be pulling out shortly."

She nodded, her hands trembling.

I walked away, blowing out a breath.

"Why was there only one?" Mama Bear asked as we headed toward the bikes. "That doesn't make a whole lot of sense, you know."

"I know," I admitted, pushing my hair out of my eyes. Though I had it in a messy bun on the top of my head, my bandana had loosened and allowed the wisps at my hairline to stick to my sweaty face. I wasn't a vain woman by any means, but I cared about my hair. I liked to keep it long; the dirty blonde locks were my trademark. "Someone wanted her across the border. She's important to someone."

"Or she crossed the wrong person," Mama Bear replied with a sad note in her voice. "At any rate, we will get her back where she belongs."

I looked back at the truck and the brains that were splattered all about the cab. "She can ride with me." While none of us were the least bit squeamish about the sight, I didn't know who I was dealing with. The realization was unsettling.

"Got it," Mama Bear said, pausing long enough to place a hand on my arm. "You all right?"

I cleared my throat. "I'm fine. Get ready to move out."

She nodded and walked away, giving me the room I needed to catch my breath.

I hated this. I hated finding women, innocent women like this, and growing more suspicious with each one that Rex and the Jesters supported it.

The man I knew, back long ago, would have never allowed this to happen to any woman.

After all, he had saved me from likely the same fate.

"Don't think about it," I growled at myself, pulling my thoughts together. That Rex, and the person I used to be, were long gone now and had been for many years. After five years, I had grown up and acquired quite a few tats depicting my stories, my own struggles.

And I'd done it all without him by my side.

My chest ached again, and I rubbed it absentmindedly, knowing it wasn't going to help. In my moments of drunken weaknesses, I allowed myself to miss him. I missed his touch, the way he made me feel, and how he'd chased away all my demons.

I missed the way he smelled, the quirky grin he would give me whenever we were joking around with each other.

Most of all, I simply missed *him*.

"Kris! We're ready."

Shaking out of the thought, I started back to the truck. *Forget that shit.* I had things that required my attention and lamenting over Rex wasn't going to help with any of it.

I joined Mama Bear and Siren at the truck, where Leigh sat drinking water.

"What do you want us to do with that?" Mama Bear asked, pointing to the drone that still hovered above the truck, watching our every move.

I grinned and pulled out my gun, aiming for the white speck with its blinking lights. "I got it."

I just hoped Rex was watching.

Chapter 2
Rex

I held in a chuckle as the screen went fuzzy and stroked my beard with my fingers. There had been no mistaking who had fired the shot that took down the drone, nor who had interrupted the shipment.

Kristina was at it again.

"What are we gonna do?" Corey 'Ironsides' Steele, asked as he leaned against the doorway of the monitor room. "That was a message, you know."

I looked up at my road captain, allowing a smirk to escape. "She's been sending messages for years now. Too bad they're always at the end of a gun."

Ironsides chuckled, a glint of humor in his eyes. "At least none of those bullets have killed you yet."

"She nearly did," I answered, remembering the scar just below my collarbone. To this day, I still couldn't believe she'd shot me. But, it was my own damn fault I'd been there in the first place.

It was just another piece of our shitty puzzle we still needed to figure out and now that she had stepped over this line, I would have to pull the trigger.

I was going to have to bring her in. The man she shot today was one of my club members, not to mention she cost me a hell of a lot of money stealing that shipment.

And I had people to answer to as well. "Round up some boys, we're going."

"You're shitting me," Ironsides said, his jaw dropping open. "You're going to go after her now? Really?"

I swallowed the bitter taste in my throat. "I don't have a choice. She's crossed a line."

"About goddamn time," Ironsides responded, running a hand over his head. "I thought I'd never hear you say that."

That made two of us.

For five years I'd let Kris and her little gang of women have the upper hand on me and mine, ignoring the jabs that she had chained me down forever, hence my nickname, 'Chains.' I took it all in stride, not denying the fact that Kris had a pull over me. "Get the guys together. I want to pull out in ten."

"Alright then," Ironsides said, walking out of the room.

I sat back in the chair, staring at the screen. I would do what needed to be done. As president of the Jesters, I had to show them we weren't going to take this lightly.

No matter how much it pained me to do so.

Wiping a hand over my face, I gave myself a minute before pushing out of the chair, steeling myself from any emotion that assaulted my body and my damn soul.

I didn't have a heart anymore.

You see, Kris took it from me, and no matter what she did to me now, she would still own it until the day I died.

But it was time to show her I wasn't a pushover.

I walked through the club, passing members who were getting shit ready to ride out. I'd been the president of the Jesters for five years now, working my way up through the ranks to be the first in line when the time came. Becoming president had been a fucking dream come true and I'd shared that with Kris, hoping she would support me in my decision.

She had, for a time, but just like all good things, that came to a crashing halt. Since then, I hadn't spent any time with her outside of her fucking shooting at me. She'd gone and created her own club, for which I was damn proud of her, but it didn't make me less worried she'd get herself killed.

Not even after five years.

Walking outside to my bike, I dropped my shades over my eyes to block out the bright sun. The club girls milled around, giving my guys one last wave or a kiss in case they didn't make it back. While I hadn't forgotten about Kris and what we had shared, I hadn't exactly remained celibate either.

In fact, one of those club women was draped over my bike, her red lips formed in a pout as I approached. "I thought we were going to have some fun this afternoon, Chains."

I reached around, my hand on her waist to lift her off the bike, grinning when she wrapped her long legs around my waist, refusing to let go. "Come on, Lisa. I don't have time for this."

"You never do," she said, running her long fingernails through my beard. "Hurry back, will you? I'm dying for a ride today."

I pushed her away then, swatting at her ass as she stepped away. "I'll think on it."

She gave me a heated look as I swung my leg over my bike and fired up the engine. The roar of the bike shuddered through my body, like a purr to my soul. I'd ridden since I could walk; my dad was a bike mechanic who did all sorts of work for some of the older clubs throughout the years. I grew up in that world and so it was natural for me to fall into one the moment I turned eighteen.

I was a cocky bastard and after a few licks by some of the older guys, I'd won their respect by perfecting my shooting and knifing skills. It was all preparation for the moment I would be president of my own club, a moment I saw realized five years ago.

The guys under me, they depended on me to make good decisions for the club and keep up relationships that funded us, too.

And Kris, practiced from years of my tolerance, was starting to cut into our profits. I couldn't allow it to go on. She'd hit five trucks this month, and I'd spent the better part of the week covering my ass from the Pacifica Cartel.

I maneuvered my bike to the front of the small pack that would run with me, grabbing the horn that waited for me to give instructions.

I had only one. "We take them alive."

The rev of the engines rewarded me and we took off, tearing down the highway. I knew Kris would head back to her clubhouse to celebrate and I planned to be there to crash her party.

***

Thirty minutes later, I pushed away from the doorway as Kris pulled up into the drive and cut off her engine. Back then, I'd been fucking serious about her. Now, I wanted to wring her pretty little neck.

"We're here," she said to her passenger, waiting until the young woman climbed off the bike before she swung her leg over and stood on the driveway. I watched her every move, my eyes drinking in the way her jeans molded to her legs, and the black leather vest stretched tight across her breasts. Tattoos covered her arms, cutting off at the wrists right before her bare, elegant hands. *Damn, she still looked good.*

I knew she also had a small rose right above the dimple in her back and my initials on the inside of her ankle. Or at least she still had them there five years ago.

Of course, the only way I would see them now is if her legs were wrapped around my neck, and not because I was giving her cunt the best damn tonguing of her life.

She came to stand just a few feet from me, crossing her arms over her chest, her blue eyes showing no emotion or surprise. "Rex."

"Kris," I answered, giving her a nod. "You're looking good."

She didn't flinch. "I imagine you didn't come all this way just to tell me how I look, did you?"

"Afraid not," I said, my eyes searching for any injuries on her body. Damn, she looked good. "You shot at my drone."

"I didn't shoot *at* your drone," she remarked, her lips lifting in a small grin. "I shot *down* your drone. I hope it was expensive."

"It was," I answered, wanting to crack a grin myself. Kris was such a smart ass, which was one of the many, many reasons I'd loved her.

The smile disappearing from her face, she held out her hands in front of her. "Go on, take me in. Let's stop pretending you're here to talk."

Surprised, I eyed her, looking for some sort of sign she had something up her sleeve. The rest of her club also looked surprised, but none stepped forward, clearly okay with whatever their president was doing. "You're surrendering?"

"It's hot, I'm tired, and a drink wouldn't hurt," she shot back, no warmth in her expression. "So, if you're going to take me in, please stop wasting my time, so I can get out of this damn heat."

I jerked my head toward the woman near her bike, her wide-eyed expression glued to our interaction. "What about your new Prospect there?"

Kris glanced over at the woman, her mouth setting in a thin line. "She's not a Prospect. She was in your precious cargo."

I narrowed my gaze, surprised by her words yet again. The cartel hadn't mentioned anything about people being in that shipment, just guns and drugs. "I didn't know she was in there."

Kris let out a little laugh, shaking her head. "Fuck you, Rex. Tell me another lie, will you? Come on dammit, take me in and we'll talk about this."

I ground my teeth together, holding up my hand when Ironsides stepped forward to grab Kris. She was my problem, not anyone else's, and she would be going with me back to the clubhouse. He shot me a look, but I ignored it, hating he knew how I felt about her. He was the only one who had seen me in my weak moments over Kris, though I knew he would take them to his grave before he told anyone. "Fine, get on my bike."

"I'll ride with Ironsides," she shot back, dropping her hands. "Anyone but you."

"Darling, the feeling is mutual," I growled, grabbing her wrist on the way past her and dragging her to my bike. How many times had we done this? How many times had she held onto me as I tore down the highway, thinking nothing could go wrong between us?

What a damn fool I had been. "Get on."

Thankfully, Kris didn't respond, but just slung her leg over the bike. "Let my club stay. I can tell you everything you want to know."

I shifted my weight onto the bike. "The girl comes."

"If the girl comes, my VP does as well."

"Done."

"Thank you."

I heard the soft words before I gunned the engine, revving it over and over again to drown out the impact they had on me.

Shit. This wasn't a good idea.

After relaying the message to Ironsides, I felt the barest brush of Kris's arms around my waist before I took off, my body fighting back all kinds of emotion that came from that simple touch.

She was going to be the death of me.

The wind slapped my face, but I welcomed it, leaving behind my club and hers. Out here on the open road, it was just me and her, just like the beginning.

Now I had to figure out how we could have an intelligent conversation without killing each other in the process.

Chapter 3
Kristina

This was not how I had anticipated my afternoon to go, but I guess it could have been worse. Rex's motorcycle roared down the highway, back to the Rough Jester's clubhouse, and I allowed myself to lean against his strong back while the smell of leather and motor oil assaulted my senses. The smells reminded me of how he used to come to bed still smelling like motor oil after working on his bike. I'd fussed at him more than once about it but had secretly enjoyed the sense of security it gave me.

And now, God, I couldn't let go of him. Just having him this close without us being face to face with each other was calming me down, lulling me into a sense of security I hadn't felt in years. I knew every inch of the biker seated in front of me, every quirk and flaw in him.

While we'd both aged, Rex still looked like the man I had fallen in love with, that beard of his neatly trimmed and covering the lower half of his face. His ice blue eyes had bore into mine the moment I looked at him and for that briefest of seconds, I'd been lost in his gaze, forgetting we were enemies.

How many times had I looked into his eyes, seeing the same fierce devotion and love there that I felt in my heart?

The bike slowed and I pulled away from Rex, gathering my thoughts. I had to remember we were enemies and he'd just lied about trafficking a human being, a woman at that.

He maneuvered the bike up against the building and shut off the engine. The rest of the crew hadn't caught up with us yet, so it was just the two of us there, baking in the hot sun. I tried to figure out something witty to say, something that would catch him off guard and show him I meant business, but my tongue seemed tangled up in my mouth and my hands itched with the urge to touch him all over.

"We can leave you know," he said after a moment, his voice barely above a whisper. "I know where there's cold beer and good music."

My heart leapt into my throat and the sudden rush of emotions surprised me. He sounded so hopeful, and nothing like the harsh man I'd saw him becoming.

He sounded like my Rex. My savior, the man who had brought me out of the brink and back to the living, showing me that not all men were bad after all.

Well, until he dashed my dreams and I had been faced with reality.

I pushed myself off the bike, pulling off my bandana and letting my hair free to fall in waves around my shoulders. It made me feel like I had a shield against him.

Rex took his time climbing off his bike, pulling off the leather gloves he had on, the gloves I knew he wore when he was walking into a fight. "Did you really think you would need them with me?" I asked.

He looked up and the air in my lungs ceased to exist, the intensity in his eyes taking my last breath away.

"I honestly didn't know what you would do, Kris."

Fumbling to get a hold of myself, I pushed past him, walking into the clubhouse I had once called home. Not much had changed since then. The walls were still a dirty brown, the couches in the main room still run down and occupied by smelly, burly bikers whose mouths dropped open when I walked past. I kept my head held high as I passed them on my way to Rex's office.

But just being there brought back a ton of memories.

I entered the space, the faint smell of cigars Rex favored hanging in the air. The desk was the same, the chair the same, but what I hadn't anticipated seeing was the same picture on his desk, the one of us at some motorcycle rally we'd attended together to put our bikes in their contest. I was seated on his lap, his arm around my waist and we were laughing.

It was a picture of love and happiness.

"You remember that day." It wasn't a question, but a confirmation.

"Of course, I remember that day. My bike beat yours."

His laugh was rusty, but still music to my ears and I didn't turn around, not wanting to face him just yet.

"There you go, making everything a contest."

"You're just mad I constantly beat you at your own game," I answered, pursing my lips together so I wouldn't smile.

"Maybe I let you win."

"Never. That's not your style."

His hand brushed over my shoulder and I turned, pulling away from his touch. I couldn't have him doing that now, no matter how much my body craved him.

The loss on his face was easy to read as his hand fell back to his side. "It's good to have you here, Kris."

I crossed my arms over my chest, attempting to shield myself from my feelings and his words. "This isn't a social visit Rex. You had a woman in that truck. Don't tell me you aren't involved with trafficking."

He came toward me, stopping just mere inches in front of me. "I didn't know she was back there, I swear it."

Oh, how I wanted to believe him! The Rex I knew would have been appalled and championing my efforts to stop such a despicable thing from happening.

But he was working with the very club that made it happen and he couldn't deny that fact.

"So, you are saying the cartel didn't sponsor that run?"

His jaw ticked and I knew I had him.

"You don't understand, Kris."

I arched a brow. "I think I understand perfectly. Let's see, you are working with the cartel, which are the exact people who are sending women and kids over every fucking second of every fucking day, to Mexico and beyond, to be trafficked into prostitution and God knows what else. That was your fucking drone watching the operation going down, which means that was your fucking van. Tell me when I get it wrong, will you?"

Rex reached out in a flash and grabbed my upper arm, his fingers wrapping around my skin. I should have been scared, but I wasn't. My body reacted to his touch and instinctively I stepped closer.

Oh, dear God, why were my knees weak?

"You know me," he finally said, his jaw clenched so tight I thought his face would break. "I don't condone that sort of business."

"Well you're supporting it," I shot back, glaring at him. "In fact, you are all up in it and have been for years. Face it, Rex, you can't deny that fact."

He glared at me, all traces of humor or kindness gone from his expression. "I didn't know, I swear it, Kris."

I wanted his words to be true. And, I wanted to kiss the hell out of him, too, but I couldn't give in to either desire. The problem was, I didn't trust him. No matter how hard I tried, I couldn't, not with everything I knew about where his club's money came from.

That and he was unwilling to see me as an equal, even though both of our vests had 'President' on them. He would never see me as that, only as a club girl who had fallen in love with him.

Finally, he strode toward the door, giving us both some needed space. "I'll be back. Stay here."

Like I was going anywhere. I watched him leave the office before releasing a breath, glad to have some time without him in the room. My space seemed smaller when he was around and it was easier to slip into feeling like the scared woman he'd first rescued, the one who gave her heart away thinking it would all work out in the end.

It hadn't and we were both hurting because of it.

"Shit," I said, staring back at the picture on his desk. I didn't know that woman anymore and I doubted Rex knew the man either. So much had changed between us, so much had gone wrong.

But in the same breath, so much had gone so right while we were together. Biting my lip, I thought back to the night Rex had been sworn in as president, perhaps the happiest night of his life.

***

My face felt like it was going to split from smiling so much, holding up my beer for yet another toast to Rex and his new title. He stood next to me, his arm around my waist, squeezing it every now and again. I couldn't wait to get him alone and show him how proud I was of him, what he had become, and what that meant for us in the future.

"Thank you, thank you," Rex was saying, a grin on his face. "I just hope you aren't looking to string me up in a month or so."

"Nah we'll just take you out back and shoot you." Corey grinned, throwing his arm around my shoulder. "And we'll let Kris do it."

Rex looked down at me and the warmth from his eyes radiated into my body, a promise of what was to come. "I couldn't think of a better way to go then."

I grinned back at him, giving him a nod in return. I could never hurt him, he knew that. I loved him too much to ever harm him.

Corey gave my shoulders a squeeze before he moved on, surrounding himself with a bevy of club girls. I had been one of those girls, though my luck had changed somewhat since Rex and I had become an item. He had brought me here, into this family, when I needed it the most and hadn't given up on me no matter how many times I'd wanted to give up on myself.

For that, he was my hero.

"Come on," Rex said, setting down his beer. "I want to show you something."

I arched a brow but allowed him to pull me down the hall, laughing at the catcalls and hoots that followed us. He moved us into the office and shut the door, leaning against it, a lazy grin on his face.

"What's so important you couldn't do it in the room?" I teased, feeling my heart flutter at the sight of him.

The grin remained on his face as he advanced, until I was trapped between his hard body and the desk.

"You know I love you, right?"

I ran a finger down his shoulder, a giddiness coming over me every time he told me that. "You might have mentioned it a time or two." I didn't know what was going to come out of his mouth and suddenly I was nervous about the possibilities. What if he proposed tonight? We'd been together two years, longer than most couples in this line of business, and it was naturally the next step.

Was I ready?

He laughed, brushing his lips over my forehead. "You are absolutely the hardest woman to get a rise out of. I mean, could you at least melt against me or something?"

I pushed at his shoulder until he stood straight, dropping to my knees with a saucy smile on my face. I didn't know what he wanted to do tonight, but I knew what I wanted to do. "How about I show you, Mr. President, what I can do?"

"Kris, wait," *he protested as I reached for his belt buckle, his hands on mine to still them.*

But I cupped him and he groaned, his hands finding their way to my hair and I knew I had won.

It wasn't until much later I realized we'd never finished our conversation.

***

"What are you thinking about?"

I shook out of the memory, glaring at him. "Don't sneak up on me like that!"

Rex handed me a bottle of water, still chilled from the fridge. "I thought you were thirsty."

I unscrewed the top and took a long swallow, attempting to wipe the memory from my mind. That night had been mind-blowing, the two of us lost in each other.

We would never be like that again, and it made me sad to even think about it.

Chapter 4
Rex

She looked guilty.

I watched as she took swallow after swallow of the water, wondering how long she had been out there in that desert, waiting for the moment to burst my bubble by stealing my shipment. Her clothes were covered with dirt and dust, and I could see flecks of sand on her face.

But she still looked fucking gorgeous. This woman, she was my Achilles heel, my weakness above anything else in this world.

The problem was, however, that we couldn't co-exist anymore.

I looked over her shoulder at my desk and wondered if she had seen the picture. It was right there, plain as day. What had she thought?

Was she wondering why it was still there?

Hell, I wasn't sure why it was still there. It'd been five years, five fucking years, since broke up and even the last few months hadn't been so hot between us. Sure, the sex was always there, the attraction hard to ignore, but the fighting had trumped it all.

Shit. Why had I brought her here?

"So," Kris was saying, screwing the cap back on the water. "Where do we go from here?"

I crossed my arms over my chest, attempting to glower at her. "You need to back off." Knowing she was out there, playing in a dangerous game, kept me up at night. All I could do was picture her with a bullet in her back, bleeding out with no one there to help her.

It fucking killed me.

Kris let out a laugh. "*Back off?* Really? That's the best you can do?"

I narrowed my eyes, letting her see the irritation in my expression. "I'm not joking, Kris. You could get killed."

"Oh, I see," she shot back. "You don't think I'm capable of handling a gun or actually making a difference with what I am doing, is that it?"

"Kris," I warned, the familiar argument rising up. How many times had we argued about the same thing years ago? But it was even worse now. I didn't expect her to be a housewife by any means, but taking on the Pacifica Cartel? Hell, the Mexican government couldn't even do that.

"What, Rex?" she said in a soft voice. I remembered that voice all too well. She was irritated, maybe even a little hurt by my words. "You never have seen me on the same level as you, no matter what I do, what I have done to prove myself over and over. I am damn *president* of my own club. Mine! Not yours, not anyone else's. People, they trust me, my decisions, but you won't look past the fact that I'm a woman!"

"You're not just *a woman*," I growled, the prick of my anger starting to grow. "You were mine."

Her eyes widened briefly and I realized what I had said. She wasn't my woman, not anymore, and hadn't been for quite some time.

"I'm going to pretend you didn't just say that," she said tightly, clear anger in her voice.

"Dammit, Kris," I said, trying to rein in my anger. We didn't need to argue about what she could and couldn't do. Kris was perhaps the most amazing woman I had ever met, the only one who had turned my head and stolen my heart in the process. It was my job to worry about her and what she was getting into. Didn't she understand that? Even though we weren't together any longer, it didn't mean I didn't care about her or what she was into.

I cared too damn much.

Kris held up her hand. "So, can we just talk about the situation at hand? I don't want to go down that road again."

I didn't either. "Fine. You have to stop attacking these shipments. You're lucky your club hasn't been injured or killed in these raids."

She arched a brow. "You're doing it again."

I shrugged. "So, sue me. But tell me I'm wrong."

Kris sighed, rolling her shoulders. "Fine, we can agree to disagree I guess, but I'm not stopping. You know what would have happened to her if I hadn't taken out that shipment today. You can't deny it."

She was right. I couldn't, but I hadn't known that woman was in the back of the truck. When we'd packed it earlier today, there was no woman in the back. I couldn't explain it and I knew she didn't believe me, but it was damn truth. "You're getting bolder."

She grinned, nearly taking my breath away in the process. It was her devil-come-get-me grin, one that had always told me she was up to no good.

That and she loved to look at me like that in bed, right before she would, well, this wasn't the time nor the place to relive those memories. I took a step toward her. "I don't want to scrape your pretty ass off the pavement because you attacked the wrong one, Kris."

"You won't," she said. "I can take care of myself."

"I know," I said. Hell, I had taught her to shoot and fight myself. "But that doesn't mean you won't get shot or killed."

Instead of flying off the handle, her gaze softened, and she let out a little noise. "What happened to us, Rex?"

A moment of weakness for her. My body went into complete overdrive, my blood simmering just under the skin. These moments were a rarity, even in the time we were together, where Kris would show her soft side. I knew why she preferred the other side of her, the one who didn't take shit or give a damn.

I knew all too well, but I did like to see the vulnerability in her, too. For a ball buster like her, she could make a man feel like damn superman when she was like this. I took another step toward her, reaching out to smooth a flyway hair that stuck to her face.

She had no idea what she did to me.

Her mouth parted and I licked my lips in anticipation, my thoughts scattering as I prepared to kiss her. She had kissed me once since we broke up. One time. Right before she shot me.

"Rex," she said, her hand landing on my chest, holding me in place. "I…"

"I know," I finished for her and dipped my head.

"Rex, Kris."

She jumped so far back away from me at the sound of Ironside's voice that she ran into the desk, rattling the things on the surface as I turned toward him, wanting nothing more than to shoot his ass dead. I had gotten so close, *so close*. He arched a brow, but I shot him a look, daring him to say anything.

He knew my weakness and she was right behind me, but I didn't want to hear it right now.

"What?" I barked out.

"The girl, she says she wants to talk," he said as Kris slid in next to me, her expression stone cold.

"Call a meeting," I ordered. I was just as interested in how she'd gotten in the back of that truck as Kris was.

And maybe she would help bolster my stance that I had nothing to do with her being there.

"I want to come, too," Kris said, clearing her throat.

I gave her a sidelong glance. "And why should I jump at your command?"

She matched my stare. "I found her. I rescued her. I deserve to hear her out."

Well, she had me there.

"Besides," she continued, tossing her long hair over her shoulder as she looked at Ironsides. "I'm a president too. It's courtesy."

Ironsides choked on his laughter. "I will go call the meeting. You two can fight this out."

I waited until he exited the office before I rounded on her, not believing the balls she had. "You have no right. I could forbid you."

She gazed up at me, giving me a sickly-sweet smile. "You could, but then I would just bust up in there and embarrass you in front of your club, Mr. President. Is that what you want?"

I took a step toward her, knowing I wasn't intimidating her in the least. She could see straight through me just like I could her. After all, she had seen me pissed off before and I was far from it.

Another few minutes in her presence, and I wouldn't only have a permanent hard on but also blow a damn gasket. "It wouldn't be the first time."

Her cheeks flushed and I knew she was thinking about the last time she had barged in on my club's business like she owned the joint. That had been our downfall among a shit load of other things.

I'd been trying to control Kris since the beginning and failed. What made me think I could do it now?

Chapter 5
Kristina

I had to get out of here. I felt like a rat caught in a cage, unable to breathe, unable to think.

Rex was far too close, that was it. I never could retain control of both my mind and my body whenever he was around.

And he was making me remember all these memories, memories I had attempted keep buried for years.

Like barging in on his meetings, for one. I had ruined one before, a big one that had the other club members teasing him about me having a grip on his balls.

He didn't talk to me for two days afterward.

It was the one and only time I'd regretted something. Okay, maybe not the one and only time, but it was on my list of things I'd screwed up. In that moment, I had been so mad at him for not involving me in club business because he spoke to me like an equal when we were alone. But looking back, I'd realized no matter how he was when no one else was around, he had no plans to change everyone else's perception of me as just a club girl.

"I apologized for that one."

He let out a harsh laugh. "Yeah, you did and then you were gone two weeks later."

I cringed. Yeah that was right, too. "That's neither here nor there. Are you going to let me be part of this or not?"

He sighed, finally dropping his guard enough that I could see the exhaustion on his face. I didn't want to care, not in the slightest, but it was in my being to care.

Especially for him.

"You look tired."

"I am," he bit out, clearing his throat. "But that's neither here nor there. Do you promise to keep your trap shut?"

My concern vanished into annoyance. "I can, maybe."

Rex didn't budge.

I let out a sigh. "Yes, I will keep my mouth shut, alright?"

He stared at me for another minute before shaking his head. "I'm gonna regret this, I know I am. Wait here. I have to warn Ironsides."

Elation bubbled up inside me as I watched him walk out, wanting to throw my arms around his neck and kiss him senseless. I guess I hadn't really expected him to agree to it. Could this be a turning point with him? All I had ever wanted was for him to see me for who I really was. I hadn't been just a club girl back then. I had been his partner, the one person besides Ironsides who had his back through and through.

He should have trusted me a hell of a lot more.

I tucked my hair behind my ears, brushing the dirt off the vest I proudly wore every day. Of course, today I hadn't worn anything under it except a thin cami, knowing we would be out there in the desert.

Now I wished I'd worn a shirt under it or something. Less clothing and more skin didn't exactly scream 'not a club girl anymore.' No matter how much I grew my own club, or how much my girls respected me, the guys here would never see me any differently and I hated it.

They didn't need to like me, but I needed them to take me seriously.

And what happened between Rex and I hadn't helped the issue whatsoever. Sure, I'd left him, just packed up my shit one day and walked out without word. He hadn't called, as if he had seen it coming, though by the way we were fighting, anyone could have predicted it.

I just… I couldn't take it any longer and I wasn't going to apologize for it, not to anyone.

Hugging my waist with my arms, I hoped Rex was going to keep his word tonight. I wanted to know why that girl was in the truck, what involvement the Jesters had with her kidnapping, and what the plan had been. Rex's apparent agitation at supposedly not knowing she was in there did put a small, nagging doubt in the back of my mind that maybe he really hadn't known.

Still though, I had to act like he had. I couldn't exactly take him at his word when women and children were being sold as slaves. How would that conversation go with my club? 'Hey, we're going to rein in the hits, girls. My ex says he didn't realize what was going on all these years.'

But beyond that, there was another reason, one I didn't want to think about much less admit.

If he really was in the dark, if he didn't support what appeared to be happening right under his nose, then he wasn't the enemy I thought he was. It would be a lot harder to keep the wall up between us and keep pretending to hate him even though I knew I couldn't.

I wouldn't have a reason to push him away.

And then where would I be? Where would I belong?

If I let him in again, I lose the identity I'd built. Separated, no one saw me as just another girl. No one labeled me as Rex's girl.

But if we somehow managed to get back together?

Being a club member's girl put her just above his bike in importance… sometimes. And I couldn't stand the thought. When I was in that category, my opinion, my very existence, didn't seem to matter. No matter how hard I tried, Rex never saw past the woman who slept in his bed at night.

Maybe the guys saw me as the enemy, as the one who caused them a hell of a lot of trouble, but at least I wasn't invisible anymore.

I couldn't go back to him now. Too much had changed. I had to keep reminding myself of that. If I let down my guard even for a little bit, well, I'd almost let Rex kiss me tonight.

That would have been disastrous. Of course, it'd been my body craving the familiarity of him, begging me to let it happen. It was like my cells were urging me on, rooting for me to join with the devil once more.

I shouldn't be so, well, so bitter. Rex loved me. I knew that, though I sometimes wondered how deep his love truly ran. But for someone putting up with my shit for the past five years, he had to have some love for me.

But I wanted more than just love. I wanted respect, from him specifically. Screw the club. I couldn't care less about the Jesters. They weren't my family anymore. Hell's Bitches were and when I walked into that room tonight, I would be representing them, not anyone else.

It would do me some good to remember that.

Footsteps sounded down the hall and I squared my shoulders, pulling my act together.

I was strong.

I was the badass bitch they had learned to hate.

I could eat that damn room alive.

Rex's form filled the doorway and I caught my breath, emotions swelling up in my body again. Damn him and damn my own pitiful heart.

"What?"

I shook my head. "Nothing. So, what's the verdict?"

His expression didn't change. "I need you to remember a few rules, Kris."

I put a hand on my hip. "Fine. Lay them on me."

Rex held up a finger. "One, this is my fucking club. I am the president here, not you."

I swallowed. Oh, I knew that all too well. "Go on."

He held up another finger. "Two. We are gonna listen to this chick's story and then I decide the next steps, not you, understand?"

I didn't like that one so much, but I'd agree for now. Intentions could change, right? "Alright, what else?"

"Three," he said, showing his fingers to me, "you are a guest here, Kris. This club, they want to take you out back and shoot you dead, do you understand that? You have no friends here, not anymore."

A shiver ran through my body. Rex was right. I'd burned those bridges the moment I hit their shipment the first time. Not to mention the fact that I had broken their president's heart and abandoned the club in the same breath. The only person who still even acknowledged my presence was Ironsides and I knew he wouldn't hesitate to shoot me given the chance.

Realizing he was waiting on my response, I straightened. "I don't need friends in *your* club, Rex."

A muscle flexed along his jaw, but I didn't care. It was a fair jab.

How many times had he told me the Jesters were his club and I had no right to know their affairs?

"As long as you know," he finally said, his voice tight.

The tension in the room was so thick you could cut it with a knife. I wanted to be away from there, out of Rex's intense gaze, and in a place where I could sort through my feelings.

I didn't want to be so close to him. "Can we get this over with now?"

He cracked his knuckles, something he did when he was anxious. "Yeah, let's get this over with."

I gave him a half smile, though inside I felt nervous and miserable at the same time. "After you, Mr. President."

Chapter 6
Rex

I saw the looks as we walked into the room together, knowing I would hear about this more than once after tonight. The desperation in those beautiful eyes of hers had finally worn me down. This shit, it was important to her, and I knew how much she'd worked to get herself where she was today.

I would give her this one pass.

"Order!" Ironsides said, banging on the table. "Shut the fuck up, assholes!"

The room quieted. The woman sat in the center seat at the table, right across from my chair. I wanted to know who the hell she was, how she had gotten into that truck, and why.

I just hoped she didn't throw the Jesters under the bus in the process and give Kris yet another reason to hate me.

Pushing my way through the crowd, I took my seat, noting Kris had taken up residence in the back of the room. Well, at least she wasn't demanding I give her a seat at the table, too.

Another woman stood beside her, giving me some hope that maybe she could keep her president's pretty little mouth shut while I conducted my business.

This was my house, not hers, and it was best she remembered that.

Ironsides took his seat and I folded my hands on the table, looking at the captive woman in front of me.

"Alright. We are here to hear her story, but first, if any man has any notion of how she got there in the first fucking place, I would like to hear it."

Slowly, I looked around the room, barely registering Kris's shocked gaze as I looked at each one of my men present, most in the higher ranks of the Jesters. I surrounded myself with loyal guys, not just the ones who had the means to kick ass. I wanted to be able to trust them, and so far, none had let me down. I didn't think any of them had put that woman in the back of the truck.

Still, though, I had to ask. "Alright," I finally said after it was clear none of the Jesters had any intel. I nodded to the woman. "The floor is yours. We need to know everything."

She swallowed, her eyes travelling around the room at the burly men surrounding her. I hoped she wasn't some sort of victim, because no matter how much I hated to admit it, Kris had stopped something terrible from happening to her.

To my surprise, she straightened in her chair, resting her arms on the table. "My name is Leigh, Leigh Greene. I am a kindergarten teacher here in Castillo." She then looked over to Kris. "And thanks to you, I will be able to return to my class."

Kris gave her a nod and the look on her face made a dash of pride spurt through my body. Despite how bat shit crazy she made me, Kris had done something many women wouldn't even consider doing. It was especially impressive given what she had gone through.

And she had succeeded.

"Well," Leigh said, licking her lips. "I am also the girlfriend, I guess ex-girlfriend now, of the chief of police, Brad Walker. I guess you know him?"

Well shit. "We've met a time or two." Brad Walker was a spineless bastard who loved to stick his nose in our business. I refused to pay him off, though I knew that was what he wanted, and dealt with him as little as possible. He had busted us for everything, from parking our bikes on the road to throwing a couple of my guys in jail overnight for not passing a bogus field sobriety test. They weren't drunk and their blood alcohol levels were zero, yet he still busted our asses for weeks afterward.

Like I said. Spineless bastard.

"Then you know what he's like," she said, her mouth set in a firm line. "And he's dabbling in business with the cartel."

"Fuck," Ironsides swore under his breath.

I couldn't help but agree with his sentiment. If he was affiliated in any way with the cartel, that meant we could possibly be working together, and I had no intentions of working with him.

Not only that, he could sway the cartel to drop us and then Walker could go after us with real charges that could lock us up for decades. After all, if the cartel owned the cops on this side of the border, what use would they have for a bunch of outlaws like us?

"I didn't know," Leigh continued, her expression turning sad. "Brad wasn't always a bad guy. For the first few months, he was really sweet, and I thought I had found the one, you know?"

Her cheeks flushed then as she must have realized she was talking to a room with ninety nine percent men in it and cleared her throat, ducking her head as she did so. "Anyway, I came home early one day from school when he thought I had a meeting and saw him talking to this man I had never seen before."

"When was this?" I asked.

Leigh scrubbed a hand over her face to wipe away the tears welling up in her eyes. "I think two days ago? I-I don't know. They... Brad knocked me over the head with something and I don't remember anything until I woke up in the truck."

"That truck was packed for shipment last night," Ironsides said. "I oversaw it myself. She wasn't in there."

"That means he put her there then," I surmised. That meant Walker had snuck onto our property and slid his girlfriend amongst the boxes. Even more alarming was that he'd known when to do it so that she wouldn't be discovered.

He had just complicated the fuck out of our relationship with the cartel.

Ironsides leaned forward. "Did you see the guy? Would you recognize him again?"

"Oh yes," Leigh answered, a light in her eyes. "He wouldn't be hard to miss. He had teardrops on his face and a tattoo of the virgin Mary on his neck."

"Gutierrez," Ironsides muttered, sliding back into his chair. "He delivered the damn truck to us yesterday. He knew that shipment would be going on."

"Shit," I breathed, not believing this mess. Gutierrez was one of the commanders of the Los Aztecas, the cartel's eyes and ears on the US side of the border. Walker wasn't just on the cartel payroll, he was rubbing elbows with some high-ranking players. "What else? Was there anything you heard them say?"

Leigh shook her head. "I'm sorry. That's all I know."

I ground my jaw, wondering what I was going to do with her. It wouldn't be long before Walker would know Leigh never made it to Mexico, which meant she was in a lot of danger and couldn't go back to her life, not yet. "What safehouse do we have available?" I asked Seth "Chuckler" Owens, my Vice President and the RJMC's second-in-command.

"Two on this side," he answered, his eyes fixed on Leigh.

"I'll take her."

I swung my gaze over to Kris, who had stepped forward, her hands on her hips. Damn, I knew she couldn't keep her mouth shut.

Before I could answer, though, Mac, the oldest member of our club, stepped forward. "You shouldn't even be here so shut the fuck up and get back in line, bitch."

Kris's eyes narrowed.

My hands still rested on the table though I wanted to vault over the damn thing and punch Mac out for talking to her like that. "She's my guest," I said in a low voice, directing my attention to Mac. "I give the commands, not you."

Mac let out a short laugh. "Of course you do, Prez. You couldn't control her when she was in the damn club, and all she's been doing is making fools out of all of us since the day she left. Her and those bitches she runs with."

Kris pulled her gun out and pressed it against his throat before anyone could react. Even with her slight frame next to his six-foot-eight, she held her own without a sliver of fear in her expression. "Say it again and I will blow your ugly head off your ugly shoulders."

Mac opened his mouth and I slammed my hand on the table. "That's enough! Kris, holster your gun before we take it from you. Mac, get the hell out of here before I shoot you myself."

Glowering at Mac, Kris did what I asked, tucking her gun back into her waistband. Mac shot me a dirty look before he shouldered his way out of the room, slamming the door behind him.

I waited until I had the room's full attention again, before drawing in a breath. "What kind of protection can you offer, Kris?"

She looked at me and the initial expression that flashed across her face betrayed that I had caught her off guard.

I couldn't help inwardly smiling at the thought.

"We have safehouses of our own."

"Take her, then." I said, ignoring the rumbles.

Kris's mouth dropped open as I pushed the chair back from the table and stood.

"Are you sure about this?" Ironsides asked.

The room erupted around us.

"Yeah," I answered. "We've got to keep the peace with the cartel. As far as they know, Leigh doesn't exist." I couldn't afford a war with them. I didn't have the resources or the money to pay them off. "Dismiss this damn meeting."

"Meeting is over!" Ironsides shouted, banging his hand on the table. "Get the hell out."

I watched as my men filed out of the room, their eyes straying to Kris and her companions more than once. I knew what they were thinking. They thought she still had a hold on me, that I couldn't keep my shit together whenever she was around.

While this decision had nothing to do with either of those facts, they were true. Kris did have a hold on me.

She waited until the room had cleared before walking over. "I don't know what to say."

I leaned forward, bracing my forearms on the table. "Well let me tell you what to say. Keep her alive and out of the prying eyes of the public. Let them think you've set her free or they will come after you."

"They are going to do that anyway," Kris replied, a sparkle in her eye. "But I won't compromise my club by being stupid."

I straightened. "Good. Go on back. We're done here." I needed some time to think, some time to decompress with a few beers and maybe a shot or two before I dealt with the aftermath of today.

She hesitated before leaning across the table, her lips brushing my cheek. "Thank you, Rex."

I snorted, leaning back in the chair. "Just don't make me regret this."

Kris gave me a saucy smile as she headed toward the door, motioning for Leigh to follow her. "Now when have I ever done that?"

I shook my head, a chuckle escaping me at her outlandish statement. Regret was a common theme between us. I was taking a huge risk letting her take Leigh with her and putting a target on her back in the same breath.

This wasn't going to be the last time we would see each other, not by a long shot. I wasn't going to let this go. The cartel would hear about the blocked shipment and that was going to cause for both our clubs, no matter how much we tried to stay out of it.

"You know what you're doing?"

I turned to Ironsides. "I damn sure hope so. She doesn't need to be there, not with the cartel breathing down our necks."

Ironsides chuckled. "I wasn't talking about the girl. I was talking about Kris."

I gave him a shrug. "Time will tell I guess."

Chapter 7
Walker

Brad Walked looked down at the number flashing on his screen, clenching his jaw. As much as he didn't want to answer it, the last thing he needed was them showing up at his house, or worse, at the station. Picking up the phone, he swiped to answer it. "Yeah."

"You fucking screwed me over."

"And how is that?"

"The shipment. It never arrived and now I have to fucking answer for it."

"Shit," Brad said into the phone, running a hand through his hair. If the shipment didn't arrive, then Leigh was likely still around Castillo.

And now she knew his secrets.

"You need to fix this," Cesar was saying. "It was those bitches who stopped the shipment. They need to dealt with."

"I'll handle it," Brad said with a thought popping into his mind. He needed to ruin the image of Hell's Bitches and their leader, make everyone doubt their intentions.

Kristina Price was going to rue the day she put her nose in his business.

"You better," Cesar warned. "Or I won't be able to stop any war on Castillo ground because of it, and it will be your ass then."

He hung up and Brad threw the phone on his desk, cursing Leigh's name. There had been a time, long ago, that he thought Leigh could be the one. She was sweet, innocent, and willing to do whatever he wanted.

But that hadn't lasted as long as he would have liked. Leigh had started snooping around, even growing a damn backbone, and no matter how much he had tried to beat it out of her, she hadn't relented.

Her seeing him with Cesar was the final straw. He couldn't have her talking to anyone about the chief of police doing deals with the cartel. The community would be up in arms and he would face a formal investigation.

The money in his offshore bank accounts from his willingness to turn a blind eye to some of their dealings would only get him so far.

Leaning back in his chair, Brad thought about his next move. He had to get the Hell's Bitches to go away. He couldn't afford to lose the cartel's backing. If he did, they would make his life a living hell.

Chapter 8
Kristina

I pulled my bike up to the door, shut it off, and tugged the bandana down off my mouth and nose. My heart still raced from the meeting earlier, how I'd stood up for myself. And at the end of it all, Rex had given me a boon by letting Leigh come back with me and my club.

It was a huge win all the way around.

Climbing off, I watched as Mama Bear pulled away with Leigh on the back of her bike, heading for the safehouse on the outskirts of town. I'd already sent some of the other members over. Given who this woman was and who she was affiliated, she needed a heavy security presence.

Brad Walker. There was no love lost between me and him, having had run-ins over the years for stupid stuff. He loved to pull my bikers over for small things just to irritate us, but now I was concerned about his connections with the cartel.

We could be heading into a war.

Pushing open the door to the clubhouse, I stepped inside. Due to the lateness of the hour, there weren't many members milling around, so I grabbed my own beer and walked to the back deck that was closed off by a high perimeter fence. When I had chosen this house as our official clubhouse, I'd wanted to make it as private as possible. Some of the women were running from something, whether it was an abusive husband or a criminal history, so I made it a safe haven for all of them regardless of their story.

I didn't delve into their backgrounds when they looked to join the club, only taking what they were willing to tell us during the process. It wasn't my business as long as they were loyal and they were able to keep their personal shit out of club business. Some could, some couldn't, and those who couldn't were shown the door, stripped of their vest, and wished good luck in their future endeavors.

I didn't have time to babysit but I could understand the need to hide.

Pulling out a pack of cigarettes from my vest pocket, I selected one and lit it, inhaling the acrid smoke as I opened my beer. I didn't smoke all the time, but every once and a while it was nice to have a cigarette or two.

Today definitely warranted one.

Blowing out the smoke, I took a swallow of my beer, feeling the cold liquid slip down my throat to settle in my stomach. I wanted to get drunk, to forget about today and what had happened. The bottled-up feelings I'd ignored for five years came rushing back the moment I saw Rex.

Just when I thought I could finally push him out of my life and my heart, he popped back up like a bad pimple.

Sighing, I took another drag on my cigarette, looking up at the star filled sky. Rex Harper had been my saving grace once upon a time, when I was less tatted and very much just an innocent, dumb girl.

***

I sobbed as I clutched my shirt together, my bare feet slapping against the pavement as I ran down the broken sidewalk. I should have known something was up when James had driven me to this house on pretense that there was a party going on tonight to celebrate our high school graduation.

He didn't tell me that I was the party.

"There she is!"

I broke off from the sidewalk, feeling the ground bite into my feet as I hurried down a dark alley, hoping to find somewhere I could hide. My heart broken, my body throbbing from the assault I had just endured, I didn't know how I would face those guys if I saw them on the street.

Thank God we had already graduated.

I stumbled out of the alley, my feet on fire, and found myself on another dark street, the houses patched together and a far cry from my parents' house on the other side of town. I should have listened to my best friends about James.

I shouldn't have given myself to such an asshole.

Making a split decision to turn left, I ran down the road, frantically looking for a light on through a window or someone out on their front porch. I just... I wanted to go home and forget this night ever existed.

Finally, I saw a beacon of hope; a small beam of a light shone out from a little house and ran to the stoop, hoping I wasn't stepping into another bad situation.

Well, nothing could be worse than what I had just gone through. The hands, the jeers, the assault. The phones in my face recording it all.

I wouldn't wish it on my worst enemy.

"There she is! Come on, Kris. We were just getting started! You know you liked it!"

I kept my back to James and his friends while I banged on the door and prayed someone would answer. "Please! Help!"

The door opened and I fell against a strong, warm wall.

"Hey now, what the hell?"

I looked up to see an ice blue stare meeting my own, a frown on his harsh, angled face. "Who the hell are you?"

"I need help," I got out, tears clogging my throat. "P-please. They-" I couldn't say the words. I was ashamed of how stupid I'd been and what they had done to me.

His eyes narrowed and he set me aside, pulling out a wicked looking gun from his waistband. "Stay here."

I followed him to the doorway, watching as he stepped outside and walked down the front steps just as James and his friends approached from the street.

"You're in the wrong part of town, boys."

They drew up short at the sight of my savior and his gun, James putting on his famous grin that had roped me in. "We're just looking for my girlfriend. We had a misunderstanding and I just want to apologize to her."

"She didn't look like she wants to hear your fucking apology," he responded, tapping the gun against his thigh. "So, I suggest you get the hell out of here before I start using you for target practice."

I watched with bated breath as James contemplated this guy's words before throwing up his hands. "Fuck you, man. You can have the bitch. Come on, let's go."

I released a breath as they retreated, my savior walking back up the stairs, his eyes on mine.

"I can pick them off from here if you'd like."

I let out a half laugh, half sob and collapsed on the floor. It was over.

***

I drew a long swallow of my beer as I pulled myself out of that memory of the moment that had brought me and Rex together. I'd stayed in his bed that night, after he had taken care of the cuts on my feet and loaned me some clothes to replace my tattered ones.

And the next morning, he took me home on his bike and I was hooked. Our relationship after that night came on fast and furious, and I'd fallen head over heels in love with him. While Rex could scare small children with his gruff looks, I had seen the tender side of him.

He'd helped me get over my assault and showed me what it meant to truly be loved.

That, and I learned to enjoy sex.

I'd spent more time at his little house or the club than at my parents', nearly moving in with him toward the end.

That was, until he had proven he would only see me as a club girl and not his equal.

"I figured you would be out here."

I didn't turn as Mama Bear joined me at the railing of the deck, a beer in her hands. "How is our guest?"

"She's stronger than most would be," Mama Bear replied. "Though I think she's more worried about Walker coming after us than the cartel."

"We can handle it," I said, flicking the ash off my cigarette. "That's all we can do."

She looked at me. "What about you? How are you, Kris?"

I sighed. "I'm fine."

Mama Bear let out a rusty chuckle. "Okay, yeah, tell that lie to someone else, girl. I saw the looks. He's still in love and you are, too."

I bit my lip, letting go of my bravado. "I am. I'm not going to lie." It'd been hard to see the strain between us tonight, remembering what had been and what might have been.

Oh, I had missed him so much. Leaving Rex had felt like I cut off my own arm, and for months after I hadn't known happiness. Throwing myself into my club was my saving grace.

"Well, I'm never been one to tell you what to do," Mama Bear said, looking out over the small yard. "After all, I'm not the best at picking men myself, but I do have to admit that you and Rex are like fire and ice whenever you're together."

I rubbed a hand over my face, looking over at her. "How can I even be thinking about him when going down that path might ruin everything I've worked so hard on?"

"Oh, honey," Mama Bear sighed, patting me on the back. "I know it feels like you'd sacrifice your independence, but you have come such a long way in these five years. Carving out a spot for Rex doesn't mean you have to give all this up."

But she didn't know what we'd been through, and how the meeting had opened up new wounds. Watching him preside over his group like the president he was, it was impossible not to feel those old, buried resentments bubble up. "We can't co-exist."

Mama Bear drained her beer, setting it on the railing. "Well then, it sounds like you can't have both. Which one will you choose, Madam President?"

"The club of course," I said, ignoring the stir of indecision in my gut. I had lived without Rex for five years now. I could live without him for another five or ten, right?

"Then there you go," she said, heedless of what was going on inside my head. "I'm off to check on our guest and my kids. Just one look makes me calm."

"I'm gonna sleep here tonight," I sighed, not really wanting to go home to an empty bed again. "See you in a few hours."

"Good night," Mama Bear said, resting a hand on my shoulder for a moment before walking off.

I turned back to the sky, unable to help but wonder what Rex was doing right now. Was he thinking about me? "You are so sunk," I said to myself, shaking my head. Who was I kidding? Rex flowed through my veins like my own blood.

Ugh I hated the effect he had on me!

Draining my beer, I put out my cigarette and walked inside, heading to my small office in the back of the house. We had two bedrooms set up for new prospects, but I wanted to hide on my couch tonight, away from anyone who could potentially find me.

And interrupt dreams of Rex.

Closing the door behind, me I stripped off my vest, leaving on my jeans and boots in case I had to get up in a hurry. I worried about the backlash from the cartel and from Walker, knowing they would target us eventually.

I had to protect my club. We'd worked too hard to get where we were.

I flopped onto the couch, pulling the blanket I kept on the back of it over my body. The club was quiet, but I knew I only had a few hours before I would be up again, starting another day. Closing my eyes, Rex popped into my thoughts, that sexy grin of his making me warm on the inside. Oh, how I had loved him! He had known every inch of my body, every dip and curve his fingers drifted over time and time again. In his arms, he erased the assault from my body and gave me a new understanding of what it meant to be loved.

And to love in return.

I couldn't choose. Rex was my weakness, the one thing I could never give away.

Shit. I was in trouble.

Chapter 9
Rex

I blew a ring of smoke into the sky, watching as it dissipated into the night. Behind me, the club was rocking, country music blaring while the guys drank and fondled the girls who were in attendance. It would be hours before the party wound down since I didn't have the heart to tell them to shut the hell up.

After all, we could be heading to our deaths in a matter of days because of me.

I pulled on the cigar again, the strong smell of tobacco filling the air. Every time I smoked one of these, I thought about the way Kris used to fuss at me for smoking in the house, how she would come after me with a can of air freshener until she chased me out of our house.

It had started to feel like that anyway.

The house was about to fall down around my ears, but the rent was cheap, and no one dared to steal from Jester territory. Since that night I had rescued her from her asshole boyfriend and his friends, Kris hadn't stopped coming around. At first, I brushed her off. She was too young for me, not harsh enough to deal with the shit I dealt with in my life. I was an enforcer back then, all fights and guns, and for someone like her, it wasn't what she needed.

But she hadn't given up. There was one night, a month after she first knocked on my door, where she knocked again, but this time it was her choice.

I opened the door and leaned against the doorframe. "What do you want?"

Kris licked her lips, looking nervous. "Can I come in?"

"Why?" I asked, my cock already straining against my jeans uncomfortably. "I told you not to come around. You don't belong here."

"You're right," she answered, blowing out a breath. "I don't belong here, but for some reason, you have been all I think about, so deal with it, okay?"

I grinned, moving aside. "Then come on in."

The memory was one of my favorites. It was the first time I'd seen her spark, the one that burned brightly now.

Damn, she'd impressed me. I hated to admit it, but it was true. Tonight, Kris had stood up for herself against Mac and the rest of the room, and as much as I wanted to jump over the damn table and kill him myself, Kris hadn't needed me.

I didn't know how I felt about that. Kris had needed me five years ago, and hell, I'd needed her.

Now it seemed she didn't need me at all.

I stubbed out the cigar on the concrete, wondering what she was doing now. I let her take Leigh because frankly, I imagined she would be far more comfortable with a bunch of women than a rowdy pack of guys.

But the look Kris had given me, hell it was like I'd just given her the biggest diamond in the world. I'd told her to leave because I didn't know what to do with that look and it scared me.

Yeah, I was scared. It had been a hell of a lot easier to read Kris back in the day. This Kris… I didn't know this Kris.

Rocking back in the chair, I looked up at the sky, the sound of the party really cranking up now. There had been one time in our five years apart since she formed the Hell's Bitches, one time she and I had run into each other.

***

The sound of gunfire rattled the air as I ran through the alley, my gun in my hand. Picking up the shipment was supposed to be a piece of cake, our dealings hidden under the cover of night. A quick in and out.

But someone had gotten wind and now they were shooting at us, keeping us from the warehouse that held the shipment.

"What do you want us to do?" Ironsides shouted, returning fire over a barrel. "Do we nix it?"

"Hell no," I shouted back, pressing my back against the steel building. I'd come for one thing and one thing only, and no one was going to stop me from getting it. "Cover me."

Ironsides opened fire and I took off, my breathing harsh in my ears as I raced across the expanse of pavement to the side door. I planned to break the lock and get the damn truck out of the warehouse.

A shadow crossed my path and I skidded to a stop, raising my gun. My finger rested on the trigger, ready to kill whoever might try to stop me, but a flash of golden hair stopped me from pulling it. "Kris?"

"Rex?" her voice floated through the space between us. "Shit."

I lowered my gun as she stepped into the dim streetlight, noting she still had her gun trained on me. "What are you doing here, Kris?"

"What do you think?" she countered. "Leave now Rex. I can't let you take this truck."

"You're playing a dangerous game," I answered, showing her my hands. "Why don't we just forget the damn truck and go get some breakfast instead?"

She grinned. "Always the charmer, but I'm afraid I can't forget this one, Rex. Please, don't make me shoot you."

"I'm afraid you're going to have to."

There was a split second before she fired and the bite of the bullet knocked me to the ground.

Shit, she shot me.

"I'm sorry," she said before running away, footsteps echoing in the night.

***

I shook out of the memory, absentmindedly rubbing the puckered scar. That night, I knew Kris and I were on truly on different sides, and while I'd sustained all sorts of ribbing from Ironsides when he had found out, I knew she would have killed me if she really wanted to.

She hadn't, which had to mean something.

And now, she was back in my life. This shit she had herself tangled in would get her killed and I didn't know if I could stop it. Kris didn't want my help, but she damn sure was going to get it. I'd already set some things in motion. Two of my guys, my more discreet guys, were watching her and the Hell's Bitches clubhouse. Their sole job was to report anything suspicious back to me, and keep their mouth shut about it.

Even my council didn't know what I had done.

"Thought I would find you out here."

I looked over at Ironsides, taking the beer he held out to me. "It's too damn loud in there."

He chuckled. "Yeah, okay. I don't think anyone would believe that bullshit lie."

I held up my beer in salute before taking a long swallow. "Sounds good at least. Why are you out here instead of in there?"

"Too damn loud," he grumbled, settling into the chair next to me. "You know there are a shit load of questions after tonight."

"Yeah, I know," I answered, not anticipating anything different. After all, I had let another club's president in on a meeting and let her walk out here alive. If that wasn't enough to rile them up, then we were all going soft. "They ready to oust me yet?"

He shook his head. "Nah, not yet. They're too busy getting drunk to care right now. The question is, what are you going to do about her?"

I sighed, leaning my head back on the chair. "Hell, I don't know. She's complicated a lot of things for us."

"For you, maybe," Ironsides responded. "I'm just glad I'm not in love with her. Won't make it difficult for me to shoot her when the time comes."

I knew he was teasing, but the thought of Kris getting shot, possibly killed turned my stomach. I wouldn't be able to fucking handle it regardless of what she had done to me or my club.

"Who comes first, Rex? Just at least answer me that."

"The club," I answered. The club had been here when she wasn't, given me solace when I was suffering over her abrupt departure.

I wouldn't trade it for anything.

The Jesters were, however, why Kris had left me in the first place. I'd chosen my position, my power, over her, and she hadn't taken too kindly to it. It'd pissed her off even more when I refused to share the details of the club's business.

I couldn't do it now either, but I imagined being the president of her own club, Kris would understand why these days.

"Be careful, my friend," Ironsides cautioned as he tipped his beer back. "Things have a funny way of working themselves out."

"What do you think?" I asked, not looking at him, but rather the sky again.

"I think," he started, "that Kris has grown herself some balls over the years. I am highly impressed, as much as it pains me to say it, and hell, might even think about joining her crew over this one. Company has to be much better."

I laughed. "You're the wrong gender."

"So, you say," Ironsides laughed. "Think about it, man. Co-ed showers have to be the bomb."

"Geez, you sound like a kid off for his first run at college," I answered, feeling some of the weight lift off my shoulders. I was thinking too hard about this, about my reunion with Kris. I had bigger shit going on than all of that anyway, even though most of said shit surrounded her in one way or another.

"Well I do like wagging my cock at the ladies," Ironsides grinned. Then his face turned sober. "What are you gonna tell the cartel?"

"I doubt I have to tell them anything," I sighed, thinking about the painful conversation that would probably take place in the morning. With Walker involved, I could almost bet all respective parties had been notified and there would be hell to pay if I couldn't talk Kris into returning the stolen goods.

Minus the girl of course. I hoped she believed Leigh's story. Judging by the way she'd left here tonight, I was betting she did. I was no human trafficker; I didn't have the stomach to do that to women, and children most of all. I'd been approached many times, and every time I told them no.

That was my threshold.

But Walker had screwed that up and nearly cost me any remnants of whatever good will left between me and Kris. I didn't like the disappointment in her eyes.

I didn't like that I still fucking loved her, that I was willing to give over everything I had to have her in my arms again. She'd stolen my damn heart the night she showed up on my doorstep, begging for help, and no matter how hard I'd tried to push her away after that, it hadn't worked.

Now, I was at a crossroads. Either I could pretend she wasn't here, that my feelings didn't matter, and we could continue to tiptoe around the truth.

Or I could win her back.

If I did, though, one of us would have to yield and give up something, and I wasn't so sure either one of us was ready to do that.

Shit, what a mess.

Chapter 10
Kristina

I frowned as I studied the board, seeing several of my members' mug profiles slapped on the police bulletin.

Not because they were wanted, but because they were missing persons.

"What the hell?" Mama Bear muttered next to me. "They aren't missing."

I turned away from the board, pushing the buggy full of groceries toward Mama Bear's truck. When someone called in this morning about the posters, I hadn't believed it. Surely no one would think that the women, especially the ones who had been seen around town, were missing.

But according to the town police, they were, and worst of all, there was a statement insinuating the women were being held against their will.

Bullshit, all of it, and I knew exactly where it was coming from.

We reached the truck and I helped Mama Bear load the food up. We'd bought provisions for not only the club, but also the safehouse and our guest.

Which of course was the reason for this 'missing persons' mess.

"How is she doing?"

"As well as can be expected," Mama Bear replied, grabbing a bag from the cart. "Worried he's gonna come after her and we won't be able to stop him."

I chuckled as I put the last bag in the truck. "Well, that's a worry we all face. You sure she won't try to contact him?"

Mama Bear shook her head and pulled open the driver's side door, climbing in. "Nah, she's wishing he would drop off the face of the earth. I don't think we have to worry about that."

I shut the door behind her. "Good. I'll see you."

She nodded and cranked the engine, the truck sputtering to life. My cell phone buzzed in my pocket and I pulled it out, seeing an unknown number flashing on the screen. For a moment, I thought about Rex, wondering if he'd finally gotten around to calling about our captive.

Or even just to talk. After all, it had been a week since we'd last spoke.

Snorting, I swiped my finger over the screen. Yeah right. "Hello?"

"Kris?"

I recognized the teary voice instantly. "Jessie? What's wrong?"

Jessie Vargas was one of our newest prospects and she had potential, even with her unknown past. She had walked into the club with nothing more than a backpack slung over her shoulder and little else, making her mark with some of the members for her willingness to help out wherever she could. She was young and willing, which is what I needed, even if she had a mouth on her.

Then again, we all did.

"They arrested me," she said. "For no damn reason whatsoever. I wasn't doing anything, I swear it."

I sighed. So, this was how he was going to play it. "Hang tight, I'll be there shortly."

"Okay."

Hanging up the phone, I walked to my bike, swinging my leg over the hot seat. First the missing persons posters, now my girls were getting arrested. Clearly, I'd won a spot on Walker's bad list.

I just hoped it wasn't going to get any worse than this. I couldn't have him targeting the club with bogus charges, tying us up in the court system for years. We wouldn't be able to continue our work if he busted us every chance he got.

Firing up the engine, I peeled out of the parking lot, heading toward the police station. I had to keep my cool around Walker, not give him any reason to throw me in the slammer, too, and forcing me to call the lawyer I had on retainer.

This assault on the club meant he knew what I'd done.

Soon I was pulling up to the station, parking my bike right out front. A few cops milled around outside, watching me behind their sunglasses as I shut off the engine and climbed off.

"You got a license for that thing, sweetheart?" one of them called out as I fluffed my hair.

"No more than you have to rotate around my middle finger," I cooed back at them, causing some of the others to snicker. I walked up the stairs to the front door and opened it, the blast of cold air hitting me full force.

I hated the police station. Granted I hadn't spent much time there myself, but Rex had over our year together, forcing me to call up his lawyer and bail him out for minor offenses. A person lost all control once he entered these doors, and it made me extremely nervous to be in there, even just for a little bit.

But, as soon as I entered, a surprise caught me off guard. "Getting bailed out?"

Rex grinned at me. "Not this time. You here for Jessie?"

"I am," I said slowly, wondering how the hell he knew she was in there.

"I've taken care of it," he stated, giving me a once over. "You all right?"

I brushed him off, annoyed he would stick his nose in my business. Why had he bailed her out? Why was he asking me if I was okay?

Ugh. "Why are you here?"

He rested his hand above me on the wall, looking down at me. "I heard there was some trouble, so I came down to investigate. Thought I would help you out while I was here."

Before I could open my mouth, the door opened and Jessie walked out, her head held high.

Behind her, Brad Walker's shitting-eat grin wasn't hard to see. "Well, well, well, if it isn't trouble all the way around."

"Walker," I growled as Jessie shot me an apologetic look. "I saw your handiwork this morning at the grocery store. It's not gonna work."

He laughed. "Oh, come on, Kris. You know some of those women probably have families out there, worrying about them. I'm just doing my civic duty to let them know where they are." He glanced over at Jessie. "Like this one. She probably has a family out there, worried sick."

Jessie opened her mouth, but I gave her a look, warning her to stay silent. We didn't need Walker knowing any more information than he already did.

"What? No smart remark?" Walker continued, his grin growing. "You're getting soft, Kris."

I stepped forward, balling up my fists at my side. "I'll show you soft, you piece of shit."

"Back off, Walker," Rex said, stepping in front of me.

"This ain't your fight, Chains," Walker said, his grin slipping. "You don't want to get tangled up in this."

"I get tangled up in what I want," Rex shot back, every trace of teasing gone. "And what I want is for you to do your job and stay out of our fucking business."

Brad's eyes narrowed and I sucked in a breath, wondering if he had the balls to throw Rex into jail on some crazy charge.

But Brad backed down, shaking his head. "Go on. Get the hell out of my station."

I grabbed Jessie's arm and walked her to the door, knowing Rex followed right behind us. A storm was brewing, but today was not the day we'd see the thunder and lightning.

We stepped outside and I paused, looking back at Rex. "Thank you." I didn't know why he was here or why he helped me, but I had to say it at least.

"Two in a row, Kris," he answered with a wink. "I need to record these."

I rolled my eyes and walked down the stairs, Jessie right beside me. "What did he bust you for?"

"Rolling stop," she answered with a sigh. "I was on the back of the bike."

"Fucking pig," I said under my breath. Walker was really out to get us and as the chief of the police, he could do whatever the hell he wanted to. "Get on."

Jessie did as I asked and I did the same. But when I tried to start the bike, nothing happened.

Frowning, I looked down and saw something leaking underneath. I crouched down to see what the hell happened and saw the oil line cut clean through, oil spilling all over the pavement.

That motherfucker! This was no accident.

Straightening, I glared at the cluster of cops who watched my reaction, seeing their smirks. They had done this. My hand twitched toward my gun, but Rex pulled me back.

"Whoa now," Rex said in my ear, his grip tight on my arm. "Let's just get the hell out of here, alright? I have the truck. We'll take it to the shop."

I let out a slow breath, turning my attention away from the cops and to Rex. "Fine, let's get out of here before I blow their heads off."

***

I reached into the tool drawer, located the wrench Rex was asking for, and handed it to him. We were in Rex's shop, not far from the Jester clubhouse, with Rex's favorite band playing in the background. The entire place smelled of grease and oil, all the scents that filled my memories of Rex and his clothes.

Jessie sat in the small lounging area, watching TV, which left Rex and I alone in the actual shop. He sat before my bike, his capable hands working the cut oil line quicker than I ever could. During our time together, Rex had taught me a few things so I could take care of my own bike, like changing the oil and doing a basic tune up. For someone who hadn't owned a bike before, the lessons had become invaluable over the last few years, especially without him around.

"Hey, can I throw something out there?"

"What?" Rex asked, concentrating on the bike in front of him and not me.

"I was thinking you could get out of the cartel runs."

"Kris."

I cut him off. "Hear me out." I had been thinking about this since the last busted shipment, feeling a bit bad I'd cut off his money. "The weed from California needs to be run, too. Why not do the same deal, but with less risk?" I had no interest in that route, and it wasn't as dangerous as the cartel runs.

"What would I give them?" Rex asked, still not looking up.

"The guns," I said, surprised he was entertaining the idea from me this far. "It's a win-win for both sides. The Cali guys will appreciate getting the weed into Texas."

He grunted but didn't say anything else, and I sighed inwardly. Well, it had been a good idea to me. I really didn't want Rex tied up with the cartel, knowing one day he could be paying them with his life.

Walking over to the covered bike, I peeked under the tarp. "You still haven't gotten this thing running?"

"I've been busy," Rex said as I dropped the cloth.

I arched a brow. "For five years?"

He looked at me over the seat of my bike. "Yes. Being the president is hard work, Kris, as I'm sure you know. I rarely get time to hang out in here."

"Or you're pissed at it," I added. "Come on, tell the truth."

Rex looked back down at his work, his smile gone. "Maybe I was waiting for you."

I swallowed, my teasing evaporating. "I'm sorry."

He gave a half shrug, reaching for another tool. "It doesn't matter. Things change."

I bit my lip, watching him as he worked. For a while there, Rex had been my best friend, the one person I knew I could trust above all others. He knew everything about me, but in this moment, I felt like we were strangers.

"What are you thinking, Kris?"

"What do you mean?"

"You bite your lip when you're thinking, so what's on your mind?"

I released my lip. "I was just thinking how things are different. That's all."

Rex chuckled, his eyes on the engine. "That's an understatement. If I ask you a question, will you answer honestly?"

I trailed a finger through some dust on a countertop. "Depends on the question."

"How did I know you were going to say that?" he laughed, pausing his work. "If you could go back and make this thing work, would you?"

That was a loaded question. There were so many factors into why we broke up in the first place and not just the fact that he didn't want to see me as an equal. The club became his life, which meant less time at home with me and working on things like that bike in the corner. He would come home tired, fall asleep before we even had a chance to talk, and I would lay there, tears clogging my throat because I could see our relationship falling apart before my eyes.

"There would've been a lot of things to change, Rex," I said, deciding to take the high road. It hadn't been all his fault. I was just as guilty of pushing him away at the end, attempting to move out on my own and thinking Rex would be just fine with it.

"Yeah," he finally said. "I'm done."

It took me a moment to register that he was talking about the bike and not about us. "Oh good."

He stood, brushing his hands on his jeans. "Try not to get it cut again, alright?"

I smirked. "Sure thing."

He grinned and for a moment, my breath ceased to exist, seeing the twinkle in those eyes I knew so well. Rex wasn't every woman's wet fantasy, with a scraggly beard and equally wild hair, but he was mine.

He would always be mine.

His eyes darkened and I broke the gaze, turning toward the office to grab Jessie. I couldn't deal with this right now.

I couldn't let my heart get involved again, not with him.

I reached into my pocket and threw a few bills on the office desk. "Let's go."

Jessie followed me out of the door as Rex backed the bike out of the shop, then threw me the keys. "Bring it by next week and I'll clean the rest of it."

"I'll take care of it," I said, motioning for Jessie to get on the back as I straddled the machine. "Thanks."

"You're welcome," he answered.

I fired up the engine and took off, wanting to put some distance between me and him as fast as I could. It wasn't because I didn't want to be around him.

No, I wanted to be around him too much.

I slowed at a stop light, my thoughts jumbled. "Y'all used to be an item, didn't you?"

"That's none of your business," I told Jessie, wishing the light would change so I could drown out any more of her questions.

"Well I think y'all are a cute couple," she said before the light turned green and I gunned it, drowning out anything else she was going to say.

I knew what we looked like together. I knew how it felt to have him hold me, kiss me, love me.

And I knew what it felt like to love him.

My heart squeezed painfully in my chest and I ignored it, turning the bike toward the clubhouse.

I knew all of it, and before last week, I'd thought I could bury it deep down inside and forget anything between Rex and I had ever happened.

But now, my dreams were filled with the good times between us, the times that had brought a smile to my face now brought pain in my heart. Could I let him back in? The discussion today left the door wide open as to what he was thinking about and what he might want for the future.

I didn't know.

One thing was for sure, the war with Brad Walker was on.

Chapter 11
Rex

I walked into the clubhouse, throwing up my hand to a few of the guys as I walked back to my office, my cell in my hand. Sure enough, the green dot continued to flash on the screen, meaning she hadn't found it yet.

Kris would shoot me dead if she knew what I'd done, how I had slid the tracker device on her bike when she wasn't looking so I could keep tabs on her. It wasn't because I wanted to know every detail of her life.

It was because I wanted to protect her from any shit she got herself into.

The green dot stopped and I grinned. So, Kris had made it back to the clubhouse safely. I wasn't going to snoop on her, really, but seeing that green dot in a safe place gave me some peace of mind.

"What's got you grinning?"

I looked up from my phone, seeing Ironsides in the doorway. "Nothing."

"Yeah right," Ironsides said glancing at the screen. "Shit man, she will kill you if she finds out."

I shoved the phone in my pocket. "That's why she isn't gonna find out." I had my reasons.

Ironsides shook his head, a grin on his face. "Dude, you have it bad. *Again*. Why don't you just go over there and climb in her bed? That's what you need, the both of you."

Hell, I wouldn't want anything more than to have Kris naked in my arms. Though I hadn't stayed celibate during our time apart, nothing came remotely close to the chemistry we had in bed together. It was something special, something I couldn't shake no matter what. "What do you want?"

"Gun Jesus is here."

My thoughts shifted at the name, moving to business and not of the personal nature. Gun Jesus was our arms dealer, getting me whatever gun I requested in exchange for cash I provided him from the cartel. He was a crazy fucker, some said he was off his rocker, and had been since the year 2000. Apparently, he'd thought the world was going to end and was found out in the desert four days later, dressed like some hippie Jesus and dehydrated from the lack of water.

Ever since then, he wasn't right in the head. Gun Jesus's favorite thing to do was to spout words from the Bible, and while he was mostly harmless, I stayed the hell away from him when he had a gun in his hand.

I rolled my shoulders. "Don't say a damn word about anything, alright?"

"Got it," Ironsides said, turning down the hall.

I followed him to the main room, where Gun Jesus was already bellied up to the bar, a row of shot glasses in front of him. "Jorge."

"Rex," he acknowledged, patting the stool next to him. "Come over here. Have a shot."

I did as he asked, grabbing the tequila shot and downing it without tasting the liquid. "What brings you here?"

Gun Jesus grinned, a glass in his hand. "Well now, you should know what brought me here. I'm just trying to figure out what I should do about it."

So, he had heard about the shipments. "I'm thinking we change tactics," I started, thinking about what Kris had thrown out there as an alternative to get out of the cartel business. Though I didn't admit it to her, it was a damn good idea. It would keep the money flowing into the club and hopefully keep my head on my damn shoulders in the process.

But I had to get my gun dealer to agree to it first.

Gun Jesus arched a brow, not taking the shot. "I'm listening."

I told him the idea, leaving out the fact that my rival who caused all this shit in the first place had come up with it.

Gun Jesus listened intently before taking the shot and setting the glass down on the scarred bar top. "One question. How will you handle the cartel retaliation?"

"I'm working on that plan," I answered honestly. Hell, I didn't know how I would do it, but the more I thought about it, the more my gut told me this was the right decision.

It was the right decision.

Gun Jesus looked down at his shot glasses, and for a moment, I had a sinking feeling in my stomach. It would take some balls to go against the cartel like this.

"I'm in."

Shocked, I met his gaze. "Really?"

"The Lord works in mysterious ways," he answered with a grin. "The only pact a man must honor is the one he forged with the Almighty. Far as I'm concerned, the cartel's not it."

I grinned, slapping him on the back. "Then we are gonna do this." If I could pull this off, he would be a rich man, afterall.

Gun Jesus picked up a shot glass, handing it to me before choosing one of his own. "A toast to future endeavors. As the good Lord says, those who sow in tears shall reap with shouts of joy!"

"I can drink to that," I said, downing another shot. I sure as hell wasn't going to cry about it.

***

After Gun Jesus left the clubhouse, I pulled out my phone and searched for Kris's number, knowing she probably hadn't changed it in five years. Now that the deal was locked in, I wanted to talk to her about involving her club in it as well. After all, it was her idea to begin with.

She answered on the first ring. "Hello?"

"Kris," I said, hearing the breathlessness of her voice. Was she excited I'd called?

"Rex," she said. "What's up?"

I toed my boot in the dirt, feeling a bit nervous about how to go about this. Hell, I'd never asked her out before. "I was wondering if we could get some food together."

"Like dinner?" she asked, a cautious tone in her voice.

"Yeah," I said. "I want to discuss a business deal with you."

"Oh," she said, and I cursed under my breath for putting it that way.

Hell, I just wanted to see her in some fashion outside of our respective clubs.

"Um sure, what did you have in mind?"

"I'll come get you," I said.

"I can ride."

"Let me cart you around tonight, alright?"

"Alright. Give me an hour. I'll be at the clubhouse."

I thought about the tracker on her ride. I would know exactly where she was at. "See you then."

She ended the call and I blew out a breath, wondering when this had gotten so difficult to have a conversation with Kris.

One thing was for sure, I hoped this night turned out well for both of us, and I didn't mean in a business deal either. I wanted Kris back in my bed, in my arms, me buried deep between her thighs. I wanted to taste her skin, see the way her eyes rolled back in her head when she orgasmed.

I wanted to have her again. It was damn stupid of us to keep fighting the attraction between us, to pretend it was gonna go away like it had before.

It hadn't before, which was the problem.

"Shit," I said. Why the hell had things gotten so damn complicated between us?

***

An hour later, I pulled up in front of the clubhouse, shutting off the engine and ignoring the stares of the Hell's Bitches who lounged in the front yard. They watched me from the time I climbed off my bike to the moment I walked up to the front door.

One of them stepping in the way. "What's your business here, Jester?"

I gave her a grin. "I was invited here. You go on and let your Madam President know I'm outside."

She narrowed her eyes. "She didn't say anything about a visit."

I looked down at her label on her vest, my grin widening. "You take your name seriously, don't you, Mama Bear."

She eyed me. "I know who you are, and I don't like you sniffing around her. You already broke her heart once."

Now that was comical. "Turn that phrase around," I said, watching as her eyes widened. "Go get her and I won't set foot in the club."

"No need," Kris's voice filled the air, materializing behind Mama Bear. "Sorry to keep you waiting."

I had to do everything in my power to keep my mouth from dropping open at the sight of Kris without her vest. She wore a pair of leather pants that had my mouth salivating and a flowy top that showed off one of her tattooed shoulders. Her blonde hair hung down her back in loose curls.

Damn she was gorgeous.

"Hey," she said, pushing past Mama Bear. "You ready?"

"Yeah," I answered, giving the other woman a wink.

She looked at me through slitted eyes again, but said nothing as we walked down the walkway toward my bike.

"Didn't know you had a bear on security detail."

Kris laughed. "Don't mind her. She's just, well, she's protective sometimes. Comes from her motherly instincts."

"Well she's damn good at it." I slung a leg over the bike. Kris followed suit, pressing her body against my back and wrapping her arms around my waist. I sucked in a breath when the fruity smell of her shampoo wafted through the small space between us, reminding me of all the times I'd breathed in that scent wrapped up with her in our bed.

That was the plan, to get her back in there.

I gunned the engine and we pulled away, Kris's grip tightening on my waist when I shot toward the highway. Before long, we were coasting down the long Texan road, the sun setting behind us. Once we were out of the town, I breathed in the air, a small piece of me glad to be away from it all for a while.

After all, 'all' was what had torn us apart. Without our clubs, we were just two people who had issues and somehow found each other.

The problem was, I'd struggled to keep her with me in the end.

It wasn't long before my thoughts were cut short when we arrived at our destination, a hole in the wall bar that served the best burgers on this side of Texas.

"I knew you would come here," she remarked.

I maneuvered the bike into a parking spot, the sound of tinkering country music drifting from the concrete block building.

"Where else would we go?" I grinned, letting her climb off first before I did.

She gave me a smile and walked toward the door, pulling it open. Inside, the air was thick with cigarette smoke and the smell of French fries, the place surprisingly crowded.

We found a table in the corner, away from the rowdy bar, putting in our drink orders to the waitress who met us at the table.

"God, I haven't been here in forever," Kris remarked as she leaned back in her chair.

"Me neither," I admitted. I hadn't come because it reminded me of her and the times we'd been there together. "So, I am going to get the biggest fucking burger you have ever seen."

Kris laughed as the waitress brought our beers. "As long as it doesn't bother you that I do the same."

I grinned. "Never."

She gave me a smile and something loosened in my chest, something that had been wound tight for far too long.

This was what I had missed. This was what I needed. "So, I met with our gunner today."

She arched a brow. "Gun Jesus? Don't look so surprised. I've used him a time or two myself."

I didn't know how to feel about that. "Yeah, him. He thinks your idea is a good one."

It was her turn to look surprised. "Really? You asked him?"

"Sure did," I said, picking up my beer that was poured into an ice covered mug just the way I liked it. "He's in."

Kris let out a slow breath. "Wow. I thought… I never thought you would actually think it was a good idea."

"You mean you didn't think I was listening."

She fiddled with her mug handle, not meeting my gaze. "Well maybe that, too. You never took any of my ideas to heart before."

I hadn't, which had been our downfall. "Maybe I'm turning over a new leaf."

Kris burst into laughter, hiding her smile behind her hand. "Yeah right! Rex Harper? Do something completely out of the ordinary? That's like saying it's going to snow tomorrow."

I ignored her barb. "This will be the only time we talk about business tonight, but I am gonna need your club's backing if I do this." I wouldn't be able to take on the cartel by myself and since I was sticking my neck out, along with my club's, because of what Kris had brought to my attention, it was only right for her to help out.

She thought for a minute and I knew she was hashing it out in her head. As the president of an MC, it was hard to make those sorts of decisions, knowing you could potentially be putting the entire club in jeopardy. Every decision could be the wrong one.

"Alright," Kris finally said. "We will help, but the moment you double cross me…"

"I won't," I said. I would never leave her out to dry like that. Hell, I didn't even like that she had her own club and it had nothing to do with her being a woman or that I didn't think she was strong enough.

I wanted to protect her, but I couldn't.

***

Two hours later, I had an arm around Kris's waist when we walked out together, both of us fucking miserable from the burgers we'd consumed.

"God, I will have to run ten miles to burn this off," she remarked as I steered her toward the bike. "But it was damn good."

"I can think of other ways to burn it off," I said, testing the waters.

Kris looked up with the sexiest expression I'd ever seen.

"I want you so fucking bad." It was time to put all the cards on the table, to tell her what I wanted.

I wanted her.

"Well, well, well, isn't this interesting? If I was a betting man, I would have won this bet."

I turned toward the voice, seeing Walker standing only a few feet away from us, a cocky grin on his face. He was dressed in plain clothes, though the gun was clearly visible on his hip.

"What the fuck do you want?"

He ignored me, nodding toward Kris. "I mean I knew you got around, but damn, I didn't think you would go back for seconds."

"Shut the fuck up ,Brad," Kris shot back as I stepped between them.

Brad held up his hands, that stupid ass, cocky grin still on his face. "Whoa, I mean I'm just stating the facts. You did try this before.

Did you like his cock, honey? Is that what keeps bringing you back for more?"

I heard the little noise Kris made before I threw my punch, hitting Brad square in the jaw. He went down and I turned, catching Kris mid-flight on her way to finish the job.

"He ain't worth it."

"It's not fair you get a hit and I don't," she seethed, fighting against my hold on her.

"You're under arrest!" Brad shouted, scrambling to get to his feet.

I eyed him, not the least bit concerned about his threat. "On what grounds?"

"Striking a police officer, that's what!"

I looked at Kris. "Do you see a police officer around?"

"Nope," she said, a slow smile coming to her face. "I don't see one."

"Me neither," I answered. "Might want to get that looked at Walker. I've been told I pack a mean punch."

"Fuck you!" he shouted back as I steered Kris to my bike. Well, if dinner had to end, punching Walker in his fat jaw wasn't a half bad way to do it.

Chapter 12
Kristina

I hopped off the bike as Rex cut the engine, feeling nervous and jittery inside for the first time in a long while. He did that to me, and I liked it.

Far too much.

Instead of him taking me back to the clubhouse, he had detoured to his own house, the same little hovel that had saved my life all those years ago.

"Look," he said as we walked up the broken sidewalk together. "Those damn pansies are still growing."

I looked at the flower beds I had so carefully weeded in the year I had lived there, seeing the yellow dots in the overgrown weeds. "I can't believe it."

He made a noise and walked up the stairs, while my emotions boiled over at the sight. I had tried to make this house into a home for him, for us both, and even after all this time, that was still evident in the form of those stupid flowers. The guy at the hardware store had told me I couldn't kill them.

Apparently neither could the weeds that were threatening to choke the life out of them.

"You coming?"

I looked up to see Rex standing in the doorway, his expression closed off. Was he afraid I was going to bolt, to demand he take me home? Why oh why couldn't he at least look a bit anxious and nervous like I felt about this?

"Sure."

He nodded and held the door open, waiting until I walked inside for him to do so. Knowing Rex, he had probably already done a quick peek to make sure no one was waiting in the shadows to off him, flipping on the lights he could reach to give the house some life.

Once inside the living room, it took all I had not to break down. Sure, time had done a number on his furniture, but the same rug, albeit faded, still adorned the floor, one I had purchased at one of those fancy home decorating places to give the house some life. The throw I'd left still rested on the back of the couch, the pillows still in their place on the cushions.

And that was just a few things. It was like I'd never left.

"You alright?"

I looked up at him, knowing he could see the emotion in my eyes. "Why?"

He gave a shrug. "I don't spend a lot of time here anymore. No reason to come home."

When had he learned exactly what to say to make me ugly cry?

"Hey now," he said, mildly alarmed when I fell against him with tears rolling down my cheeks. "I can burn it all if you want me to."

I shook my head, breathing in his scent as he wrapped his arms around me and held me close. Why had all of this gone so unbelievably wrong? It was clear neither of us had ever truly moved on with our lives, my heart tied to him and vice versa.

And by the looks of things here, he hadn't wanted to push me out either.

"I-I'm sorry," I forced out, my voice muffled by his chest. "It's just, it's been a hard week."

"Yeah," he said, his hand idly rubbing my back. "There's no one else here but me Kris. You don't have to pretend."

I knew that. Rex had seen me at my worst, and at my best, and I wasn't so sure where this fell into those categories. Still, I pulled myself together and stepped out of his arms, swiping at my eyes and knowing my makeup was likely ruined.

Rex cupped my face with strong hands, and before I knew it, he was kissing me breathless, his lips roaming mine hungrily. I grabbed the front of his jacket and pulled him close, kissing him for everything he was worth, the pent-up emotions and five years worth of loneliness bubbling to the surface.

I wanted him so bad.

Rex gave me a long, deep kiss before pulling back, his eyes dark with passion. "I won't be able to stop," he said, his hands still on my face. "Give me the word now and I will walk away."

I grabbed him by the jacket again, the leather cold in my grip. "Don't you dare walk away, Harper."

His cocky grin appeared, and even with his beard, I could see the dimple he desperately tried to hide. He always used to say it made him look like a pansy boy, but I'd thought it was adorable.

"Who's bossing who around now?"

I pressed my body against his, feeling the hardness of his cock butting against my stomach. "It's been too long. I don't want to wait any longer."

His grin faded and Rex's expression grew serious. "Me neither."

"Then fuck me, Rex."

He let out a breath before his lips crashed onto mine once more. He picked me up and swung me toward the kitchen table where he deposited me. I barely caught my breath as his body covered mine, one of his hands roaming over my breasts and the other toward my pants where he slid it inside my waistband. I gasped inside his mouth when his finger found my aching nub and flicked it, sending an explosion of sensations through my body.

God it hadn't been that long, had it?

My own hands slid up into his shirt, pressing against the hard chest that hadn't changed, my fingers bumping along the ridges of his cut muscles. He chuckled inside my mouth and pulled back, so that I could see the laughter dancing in his eyes.

"I forgot," I said, giving him a grin. Rex was horribly ticklish along his rib cage.

He pressed against my clit once more and I arched into his touch. "Does that tickle?"

"Hell no," I panted, wanting him to do it again.

Rex growled and started a slow, torturous assault on the hard nub, pulling my shirt up roughly with his other hand and pressing a kiss on my lace-covered breast. I moaned when his teeth tugged on my aching nipple, biting my lip to keep from cashing out so fast.

He drove me wild.

"Come for me," he mumbled against my breast, his hand fast and furious now. "For me Kristina."

"Oh God," I whispered, feeling the pressure building. The smell of him, the way he moved his fingers, his lips. I'd forgotten how good this was.

"Let go," he urged, kissing a path back to my lips. "Let go, Kris."

So, I did. Screaming out his name, I let the orgasm take control, surprised by the force of what he'd done. My body shook with the aftermath as Rex made quick work of my pants, grasping my pushing into me.

"You're so fucking wet," he said, his voice low and rough.

I adjusted to the feel of him again.

"Damn, Kris."

I pulled on his shoulders until he was buried deep inside me, gasping when my own body clenched around him. "Yes, oh God yes."

The table started to rock violently under me as Rex pounded into me, our bodies slapping together in a frenzied rush. I screamed his name when another orgasm hit me, my body convulsing around his cock.

"Fuck yeah," he said, his grip on my hips digging into my skin as he urged me onward. "That's it."

My hands bit into the bottom of the table where I held on for dear life, allowing Rex to have his way with me.

We'd always been very good at this.

"Shit," he groaned, stiffening a minute later and emptying into me.

I panted and tried to catch my breath, my sated body feeling like jelly. How had I survived without this in my life for the past five years?

"Well," Rex said a moment later, his forearms resting on either side of my body. "I will have to tell Ironsides the table isn't safe to eat on."

I giggled, unable to help it. "Or you could let him eat on it and laugh every time he does."

Rex cracked a grin. "Now that sounds like the better option."

**

I woke with a start, confused about what had happened. The room was still dark, the sun not up just yet, but after blinking my eyes a few times, I realized where I was at.

And who I was with.

Rex slept next to me, his arm thrown over my waist like he used to do in the middle of the night, anchoring me in place. A short burst of snores came from his lips, and I was glad I hadn't woken him up with my stirring.

Oh God, I had slept with Rex. Though my brain was still processing what we had done… two, well three, times during the night, my heart knew this was where I needed to be.

Screw our past. Screw the fact that our clubs didn't get along right now. This was far more important than anything else going on.

Sighing, I watched him sleep before turning my attention to the ceiling above my head, wondering what he would think when he woke. We would have to figure this out. So many things had changed between us in our time apart, and we both had responsibilities we couldn't ignore.

Plus, he'd struck up a deal with Gun Jesus, pitting both clubs against the cartel and no doubt declaring war once word got out. There was a strong possibility we could be in a fight for our lives in a matter of days. There were discussions that needed to take place; my own crew needed briefing of the coming war so we could prepare.

I needed to get an accurate count of our gun stockpile, scout out locations we could lay traps for the cartel in case they decided to hit the clubhouse.

I needed to alert Mama Bear to get her kids out, and likely Leigh, too, since she wasn't a part of this fight.

Most of all, I couldn't waste another minute in this bed, no matter how much I wanted to do just that.

"What are you thinking about so hard?"

Startled at Rex's quiet voice, I looked over to find him watching me. "Was I thinking out loud?"

He quirked a grin. "No, but I did smell the smoke coming from your ears."

I hit him playfully and squealed when he grabbed me to pull me closer, wrapping his arms around me.

"So, tell me," he said, pressing a kiss on my neck.

"I was just thinking," I said, running a finger over the tattoo on his forearm, "about our next steps."

"Always the planner," he remarked, his breath tickling the hairs at my neck. "Can't we just pretend nothing else fucking exists?"

I shook my head, my heart heavy. "I'm afraid not. There's so much to do and not a whole lot of time to do it in."

"Yeah," Rex echoed with a heavy sigh. "I will have to call a meeting to talk about this."

"Me, too," I said, something coming to the forefront of my mind. "You understand… this isn't, I mean, this isn't an official patch-over."

"No, it's not," he answered, his voice rough. "It's a partnership, Kris. I would never take over what you have worked so hard to make. I want this to be a partnership, between both our clubs."

I let out a little sigh of relief. A patch-over was where one club combined or took over another, where patches were turned in or traded for new ones. The last thing I wanted Hell's Bitches to do was lose their identity in this partnership with the Jesters.

Nor did I want to lose mine in the process again.

"Was that what you were worried about?" he asked a moment later.

"I can't say it didn't cross my mind," I said, glad we weren't facing each other. The Jesters were far more established than Hell's Bitches, and if Rex wanted to push the issue, I would only be able to defend our territory for so long. He had more members, better weapons, and a bigger presence in Castillo.

Hell's Bitches couldn't even begin to compete. Especially not with the cartel breathing down our necks.

He forced me to turn over until I faced him, his eyes searching mine. "Let's agree right now that this thing is going to work between us. The clubs, they are second in my mind."

"Rex," I started, wishing I could believe him. The club had always been his priority, and I could say the same thing for Hell's Bitches, too. As much as I liked to pretend it didn't matter, there was no reason to lie to each other either. "Let's take it one day at a time, alright?"

He was quiet for a moment, his fingers playing with a few strands of my hair. "You do want this to work, right?"

"Of course," I said, curling up against him. "When I am here, in these moments, everything feels right."

"Even with my snoring?"

I grinned. "Even with your snoring."

His hands grazed down the length of my back, sending goosebumps scattering across my skin. "We should throw a party after the announcement, you know, like one of those mixers."

I burst into laughter, raising my face so I could see if he was serious. "Really?"

He gave me a half shrug. "Why not? They're going to have to work together anyway. Why not get them all drunk so they'll like each other for once?"

I thought about it for a minute, knowing Mama Bear and the rest of my command would kill me for this. They knew my past with Rex. They also knew my weakness for him, and they would likely think he had talked me into this partnership.

Would they see me as weak? I didn't feel weak, though I wasn't on the outside looking in either.

Well that and I couldn't think whenever he was around.

"You're thinking too hard again babe. Spit it out. What's eating you?"

I sighed. "I just think this is a bad idea. Not the partnership, but just the entire damn mess. Do you have these feelings with your club?"

"All the fucking time," he laughed, pulling me against him. "It's part of being president, Madame President."

I melted back into his warmth, deciding I could spare a few more minutes. After all, who knew when or if we were going to do this again.

"Don't worry," Rex murmured into my hair. "It will work out, you'll see."

That was what I was afraid of.

Chapter 13
Rex

"Are you fucking kidding me?"

"What do those bitches have that will give us anything over the cartel?"

"We'll be slaughtered if we go against the fucking cartel. I ain't going down with some bitch trying to tell me where to aim my gun."

"Hell Tony, you can't even aim your dick, much less your gun."

I sat back and watched my group bicker about my proposal, wondering if they knew they sounded like a damn clucking henhouse, and not a rough biker gang. Kris and I had decided to tell our clubs separately first, then bring them together after a day of digesting the information for the party.

I had barely gotten through my spill before they'd erupted, clearly seeing no reason to work with Hell's Bitches.

Well, that and the concern over the cartel. They all had valid concerns and I couldn't blame them. I couldn't tell them if or when the cartel might attack, nor could I guarantee that if they did, I would get them all out alive.

For the first time in my president reign, I worried about what we could be facing.

"Well, that went well," Ironsides muttered from his seat next to me as the group had moved on to bantering back and forth with insults at each other. "Any other plans you want to spring on me?"

I looked over at him, feeling bad about not telling him first. I hadn't wanted him to give me the look about Kris, or think this was all about her and not what was best for the club. There would come a day that the cartel wouldn't need us anymore, and not only that, if we didn't change things, we'd be working alongside Brad Walker and his crew.

I didn't play with dirty cops.

I held up my hand and the room fell silent. "I know this sounds like shit, but I have thought out every logical scenario. We can either continue to work with the cartel, which will force us to be under Walker's thumb, or we can look toward the future with the weed business and not get our asses busted every time we decide to do a run. If it's not the Bitches, it will be someone else at the end of the day."

Tony looked at me, shifting in his seat. "I still don't understand why we have to partner with them, though. Surely they can handle their own shit."

"They are women," another called out from deep in the crowd. "They like a man watching out for them."

"It's a way to strengthen our numbers," I offered up, ignoring the eye rolls from the others. "You know of anyone else willing to go against the cartel? They're offering what they got. It's a logical choice in my opinion."

"As long as we don't end up having to babysit them," another said. "Then I'm in. At least they will be better to look at than you fuckers."

A chuckle went through the group and some of the tension left my shoulders. A few were actually warming up to the idea.

"They bring their own weapons, their own supplies, and have their own clubhouse. They will keep their ranking members, just like us."

"How many are in favor?" Ironsides called out. "Show of hands."

I watched as some in the room reluctantly raised their hands, others waited to see what the guy next to him was going to do before doing the same. After a few minutes, only a few sat with their hands resting in front of them.

"I will not hand down punishment for disagreeing with me," I finally said, giving each of those men a hard stare. "But I will ask that you abide by the rules we've set. I will not tolerate our guests being treated like anything other than your fellow club member. If I hear of any shit, I will shoot you where you stand. Got it?"

I got some nods, some hard stares, and decided to let it ride for now. "Meeting dismissed."

They filed out as Ironsides looked at me, a hardness in his gaze. "Are you sure about this? I mean, this is crazy shit here."

"Yeah," I said, rolling my shoulders. "I am."

He eyed me a moment longer, shaking his head. "You slept with her. It's written all over your face. Tell me you aren't putting the club up because you are back in her bed, Rex. At least tell me that."

I leaned forward. "The deal was struck before I put her in my bed. This has nothing to do with me and Kris personally. You know this is the right thing to do. Tell me different and I will call the whole damn thing off."

Ironsides let out a long breath, resignation on his face. "No, you're right. It is the right thing to do. I just, hell, I can't believe we got into this mess to begin with. We are signing our own death warrant by going with Gun Jesus and doing business with the cartel. You understand that, right?"

I nodded, knowing the implications of what we were doing. "We will cross that bridge when we get there, alright? I just need to know you support me in this." I couldn't have my own command going behind my back and stirring up trouble.

"I got you," Ironsides said. "And you know the rest do as well. Hell, I hope this works out, man."

I hoped so, too. For all our sakes.

Chapter 14
Rex

"So, it went that well, huh?"

Kris fiddled with her beer bottle, her legs propped up in the nearby chair. As much as I would have liked to be fucking her on the kitchen table again, I was eager to find out how her group had taken the news.

"Yeah," she finally said with a heavy sigh. "I thought they were gonna string me up and get rid of me for a second there. Let's just say, it's probably not going to be my defining moment."

I let out a laugh. "Well the same could be said of me, but it's the right decision. We are looking out for our clubs, Kris."

"I know," she answered, pushing the bottle away. "But what if we're taking them to their death, Rex? What if we're wrong about this?"

I knew how she felt. I felt the same way any time I made a monumental decision for the Jesters. Deciding whether or not to work with the cartel had kept me awake much of my first year as president, thinking about the money it would bring in for the club. Not only that, the favors we could cash in on any time we needed some backup.

I was giving up all of that.

"You're questioning your decision."

I looked at Kris. "No, I'm not."

Her lips lifted into a slight grin. "Yes, you are. You have that look on your face, Rex Harper. Don't lie to me."

I returned her grin. "You think you know me so well."

"I do," she said simply, dropping her legs to the floor. She pushed out of her chair and rounded the table, pushing my hands aside so she could sit on my lap. Kris placed her arms around my neck, and the stirring of white-hot lust rose up inside me as her ass settled against my growing cock.

All day long I had thought about her in my bed, underneath me, on top of me. After five years of not having her, she was back in my life and I couldn't be fucking happier. Kris was that missing piece to my life.

I nuzzled her neck, breathing in the scent of her. "Why don't you go get in the shower and I will join you there shortly."

"Mmm," she said, arching her neck to give me more access to the most sensitive part of her. "That sounds fabulous."

I kissed her skin, my hands roaming over her back. "Well I can make you feel even better than that."

Kris laughed, pulling away from me and standing. "I will hold you to that, Chains."

I grinned, leaning back in the chair as she sashayed out of the kitchen, disappearing around the corner. I'd come to hate the name over the past few years.

Probably because it was the truth. Completely and utterly the truth.

The shower kicked on and I pushed myself out of the chair, stripping off my vest in the process.

I was chained to Kris and hell, I didn't mind it, not one bit.

Chapter 15
Kristina

I drew in a breath, trying to calm my heart rate as I fluffed my hair. Tonight, was the night Rex and I had decided to pull the two clubs together in a sort of 'party.' Fueling bikers with beer and liquor might have sounded like a risky venture to most, but it would be the only way the two clubs were going to talk to each other, and we were willing to accept the consequences if all hell broke loose.

So, we had decided to go to a neutral place, renting out The Hole in the Wall bar for one night.

The place where it all started.

Pulling open the door, loud music and cigarette smoke enveloped me, and I nearly laughed aloud when I realized I'd just stepped into a middle school dance. Hell's Bitches stood on one side of the bar and the Jesters on the other, both eyeing each other like they were going to brawl at any moment.

"Well, this is going well."

I turned at the sound of Rex's voice in my ear, my heart squeezing just a little as I drank in the sight of him. We'd decided to come separately, though I didn't know why we'd bothered. One look at us and anyone could tell we were sleeping together again. "Who's going to make the first move?"

He winked at me, slid past, and stepped into the room, motioning for the bar chicks to bring out the round of shots for both clubs. "What the fuck is this?" he said, grabbing one of the shots. "I thought this is a party! Y'all look like a bunch of pansy-ass middle schoolers."

A few cautious chuckles sounded around the room as they grabbed up the shots, then one by one held them high in the air.

"To family," Rex said, his eyes sweeping the entire room. "Because at the end of the day, family is all we have to cover our asses. May it stay that way until the end."

I held my glass high with the others, looking at all the women who had done just that for me and each other over the last five years. This was my family. "And to the promise," I said, my voice ringing out over the music, "of what is to come."

"Here, here!" Mama Bear shouted. "Let's get this party started!"

I threw back the shot, feeling the burn all the way to my stomach. This had to work.

***

Three hours later, the party was in full swing. Both clubs mingled, laughed, and danced. I could finally unwind; the relief at seeing everyone getting along allowed me to do so. This was going to work.

Rex's hand landed on my arm and pulled me away from the scene, down the hall to the women's bathroom.

"You have to pee?" I asked as he pulled me inside and shut the door.

"No," he growled, pressing me against the door. "I want a minute alone, with you."

"Rex," I breathed before his mouth descended on mine, a hot, hungry kiss that stole my breath. I grabbed at his shoulders to pull him closer, his tongue invading my mouth. I'd watched him be exactly what he had always wanted to be, circulating the room with ease while he chatted with both his guys and my girls. With his quick grin and the overflowing drinks, Rex was killing it.

Rex broke away suddenly, pressing his lips down the line of my neck. "You know," he said between kisses, "what today would have been, right?"

"Our anniversary," I sighed, my hands roaming over his leather-clad shoulders. I'd noticed that, too. How couldn't I when it was the one date forever etched in my mind?

"Yeah," he responded, pulling back to look in my eyes, his rough hand coming up to cup my cheek. "Funny how things work out, isn't it?"

"Oh, Rex," I murmured, seeing the emotions in his eyes. Despite everything that had happened to us, everything we'd been through, I still loved him and would keep loving him even if this fell apart.

He opened his mouth but was cut off by the sound of someone banging on the door. "Hurry up! We have to piss out here!"

"Mama Bear," I said, smirking. "She will break down this door if we don't let her in."

Rex pressed his lips to mine in a quick kiss before stepping back. "Then we will finish this later, you can fucking guarantee that."

Hell, I hoped so. Turning around, I opened the door to find her standing there, her drunken gaze locking on Rex. "You break her heart again, I cut off your balls," she said, her words slurring. "You got that, pretty boy?"

"Clear as day," Rex said, giving her a wink. "Let us get out of your way."

I laughed as I squeezed past her, walking back into the party, my heart full. Some of the Bitches had brought Leigh along for the party, no one wanting to miss it in favor of guarding the young woman. She sat at one of the small tables, a drink in front of her and surrounded by women who would keep her safe the entire night, just in case.

I couldn't ask for anything more.

There was, however, one thing I needed to do.

Spying him lounging against the wall, I walked over to Ironsides. "Hey."

"Hey, yourself," he said, his gaze roaming over me.

I knew what he saw; a woman who hadn't truly disappeared no matter how much trouble she caused the Jesters, a woman who had his president's balls in her hand. Though he wouldn't be as vocal as Mama Bear was, he would still protect his own to the end.

"Good party. Looks like everyone is gonna get along."

"For a while," I answered, tucking my hands in my pockets.

"You know, I haven't decided on whether or not to trust you again," he said after a moment, looking at the party. "You nearly killed him."

"And he nearly did the same to me," I shot back, keeping my voice even. "There were no winners."

"Maybe not," Ironsides said, letting out a breath. "But I will always take his side."

"I wouldn't expect anything less," I answered. "I want him safe. I want him protected."

He chuckled. "Maybe you do belong together after all. Don't worry. I would take a bullet for him, die if I have to, but my loyalties only go that far, Widow Maker."

"I understand," I said. I never expected Rex's club to protect mine or me. I wanted their help, not their loyalty.

"How's your prospect?"

I followed his gaze to Jessie, who was laughing at something one of the women had said. "She'll earn her vest soon enough."

"So, when are you gonna take off her trainee label then?"

I looked up at him, curious. "Why the sudden interest?"

It may have been a trick of the light, but I could have sworn he blushed, his eyes straying to Jessie again. Them two? Really? "You're kidding me," I started.

He opened his mouth to respond, but a commotion interrupted. One of the Jesters burst through the door. "Cops!"

"Shit," I said, looking at Ironsides. That could only mean one thing.

They were after Leigh.

"I got it," he said, reading my mind.

I met Rex's gaze over the crowd and we both made our way toward the front door, pushing it open nearly at the same time.

Sure enough, a dozen police were getting out of their cruisers and combing through the bikes out front.

Brad Walker stood in the middle of the pack; it wasn't hard to note his uniform in the dark. "Well, well, what's going on here?"

I crossed my arms over my chest. "Private party. Didn't see your name on the list."

"Huh," he stated, looking around. "Funny, I never knew the Jesters and the Bitches were friends. I thought you used each other for target practice."

"Are you volunteering for our new job opening?" Rex asked. "Because we would take you up on that offer."

Walker tapped the top of his gun, irritation evident on his face. Whatever the reason he had to come out here, he wasn't getting what he wanted apparently. "Touch me and I will have you arrested. Let me in."

"Do you really want to do that?" I asked as some of the bikers stepped outside, interested in what was going on, but pretending to grab a smoke. I knew what they were doing, and I wasn't gonna lie, I did breathe a lot easier with them behind us.

His jaw clenched. "I can go get a warrant and bust up your little party."

Rex examined his fingernails. "Do that. We'll wait on you."

Walker didn't say anything, turning around to his group behind him. "Let's go."

I waited until they left. "You know this isn't the end."

"I know," Rex said, laying a hand on my shoulder. "But we will be ready for them."

***

After the police left, the party wound down. Both clubs trickled out, heading for their beds. I did the same, though it wasn't my bed I headed for.

It was Rex's.

I beat him home, using the key I'd never given back to let myself in and stripped off my clothes in the process, leaving a trail from the front door to bedroom. I'd carefully selected my lingerie, picking a fiery red bra and thong combo I knew would drive him wild.

I was nervous though I didn't know why. We'd had sex thousands of times, but tonight I wanted it to be special.

Well, or it was the alcohol thrumming through my system. Either way, I wanted to make it memorable.

By the time Rex entered the room, I was leaning against the bedframe with one leg propped on the mattress. "It's about time you came home."

"I rode as fast as I could," he said, his eyes roaming over my body. "But had I known this was waiting for me, I might have pushed the bike to the brink."

I gave him a saucy smile, trailing my nails over my leg. "Well maybe you should do that to me."

His wolfish grin heated my skin. "Oh, I plan to, right fucking now."

My heart racing in my chest, I dropped my leg and moved in front of him. "Let's get rid of some of those clothes."

Rex went rock still as I pushed his vest off his shoulders, letting it fall to the floor. Tonight, it was about me and him, not the clubs, not the cartel.

No one.

Easing up his shirt, I let him pull it over his head, exposing his hard body dotted with scars, a body I knew better than my own. There was one scar that stood out to me, one we hadn't discussed yet and as my finger drifted over the bullet hole, Rex shuddered.

"You know I could have killed you that night," I whispered.

"I know," he said. "A few more inches down, you would have."

Leaning over, I pressed my lips to the puckered scar. "I'm sorry."

"Don't be," he growled, his hand smoothing my hair. "I'm not."

Instead of pulling back, I lowered my lips to his chest, my hand grazing his abdomen. When I reached for his jeans, he drew in a sharp breath, stilling my hand.

"I need to touch you."

I looked up, capturing his gaze. "But I want to touch you first."

"You're playing with fire, Kris."

"Don't I always?" I teased, dropping to my knees. His jaw clenched but he released my hand, allowing me to continue my assault on his body. Yanking on his jeans, I pulled them down over his hips, his thick cock springing out.

With one hand, I grasped him, feeling the velvety warmth against my skin. "I want to taste you," I said, feeling a pool of wetness growing between my legs.

He gripped my hair, urging me forward. I took him into my mouth and Rex groaned, his hand tightening. This was when he was at his weakest and he trusted me, completely.

So, I brought it all back for him, kissing and sucking every inch of him until he made me pull back, his breathing rapid. Soon, he hauled me to my feet and backed me toward the bed, Rex's heated gaze on mine.

"You know," he said, pushing me back on the bed, "you are the only one I let do that to me. The only fucking one."

Oh, I knew it. Reaching up, I cupped his beard covered cheek, knowing the love shone out my eyes. How had I lived without this man for the past five years?

He grinned and slid down my body, not even bothering to tease me. When his mouth covered my mound, I arched against him, feeling the wetness through the scrap of lace I had on.

"You taste fucking awesome," he said, his finger hooking the lace and sliding it aside. "I want more."

I whimpered when he spread my folds and his tongue delved in, finding my clit and circling around it so lightly I thought I would lose it right then and there. I clenched my hands in the sheets as his hand slid under my ass and pushed me upward to give him more access, opening me to him.

It was intimate, it was raw, and it was all I ever wanted.

When I couldn't take his assault any longer, I let go, screaming Rex's name while the orgasm racked my body, trying to pull away from his tongue as he lapped up my release. I wanted him inside me, I wanted him to take me to that place only Rex could take me.

"Fuck," Rex said as he pulled back, his eyes on me. "You're fucking gorgeous, Kris."

"Please," I said, reaching for him. "Please."

Rex shed the rest of his clothing and climbed on top of me, ripping my thong off my body and throwing it across the room. I bit my lip and he posed over me, my body primed and ready to take him.

The man I loved.

But to my surprise, he leaned down and pressed his lips to mine, the scent of my release on his skin. "I love you," he whispered against them. "Until the day I die, I love you and only you."

Tears sprang to my eyes as he entered me roughly, filling me to the core. I arched against the fill of him, my body adjusting to the weight of him, the sensation of him inside me. He picked up my hips and pulled out a little, slamming into me again. The explosive orgasm overcame me, making me cry out and shake my head back and forth while he did it again and again. He wasn't hurting me but claiming me as he had all those years before.

His pace increased and I lost all sense of reality, my body floating somewhere between being completely sated and wanting more.

I wanted all of it.

I wanted Rex to let go.

And let go he did. With a roar, he poured into me, his body jerking with such intensity that I thought he would fall over.

But instead he fell onto me, my fingers stroking his sweaty back as we both fought to catch our breath. We had let it all go this time, not holding anything back, and I knew it was a new start, a chance for a new beginning for us and our clubs.

"Shit," Rex grumbled against my shoulder. "I will have to buy you a new pair of those hot-ass panties."

I grinned, pressing a kiss to his own shoulder. "Don't worry. I have a whole drawer full."

Chapter 16
Walker

"Are you shitting me? You don't see a problem with this?"

Brad sighed, running a hand through his hair. "Of course, I fucking do. I've pressed them but all it seems to do is blow up in my damn face."

Cesar shook his head. "Well, it's not good enough. The routes are drying up and the cartel wants their damn guns over the border. What's stalling this shit?"

Brad looked out of his living room window, a frown on his face. When Cesar had shown up unexpected tonight, Brad had anticipated it would end with a bullet in his brain. The gun strapped to his hip would only buy him time; if he killed Cesar, likely a car full of guys waited outside to take him out.

But he hadn't been ready for this visit. Pissed off that all of his plans weren't working, he had been in the midst of trying to find something that would work, something that would break apart this newfound shit show between the Jesters and the Bitches. Taking out their respective presidents would likely do the trick, but he wasn't ready to make that commitment yet.

"This is your fucking problem," Cesar was saying. "And you have to clean it up."

"I'm trying," Brad insisted, his eye on Cesar's hands in case the man went for a weapon.

"It's not good enough," Cesar bit out. "It's time for action."

"What kind of action?" Brad asked, feeling the invisible noose around his neck tighten.

Cesar grinned. "We send a message."

Brad nodded, not liking the look in Cesar's eyes. As long as it didn't turn out with him dead in the desert somewhere, he would do it.

A few days later, he found his opportunity. Brad flipped his lights on as he came up behind the biker, noting the flaming red hair streaming behind her in the wind. His cock swelled and he tamped down the thought, attempting to keep the task at hand in the forefront of his mind.

He had to do this.

She pulled over to the shoulder and he cut off his radio. There would be no calling in plates with this one.

Climbing out of the car, he left his hat, drawing his service weapon in his hand as he approached her. "Turn off the bike!"

"What did I do?" she shouted back, killing the engine.

Her eyes had barely strayed to the gun in his hand when he shot her, not giving her a chance to react. Woman and motorcycle toppled with a thud. Brad holstered the gun, picked her up, and threw her over his shoulder.

Neat and easy. That was the way he liked it.

Opening the trunk, he dumped her in, giving himself a minute to take a good look at her dead body. Damn. She was actually hot. Under normal circumstances, he might have had her suck his cock or something, but orders were orders.

Shutting the trunk, he walked back to the bike, pulled the key out and flung it into the desert. Hopefully it would look like someone had abandoned their bike after a crash.

Maybe Brad would even send out one of the patrols this way tonight, so that someone else could call it in and get it towed.

A smile spread over his face as he walked back to the car, whistling.

It was time to send that message.

Chapter 17
Siren

Siren pulled up to the clubhouse and shut off her bike, glad to be done with the ride for now. Her face was windblown, her arms burned from the blazing sun, and all she wanted was a cold shower and an equally cold beer.

Stretching her legs, Siren walked up to the front door, not at all surprised to see a box waiting there. Mama Bear was forever sending her packages to the club and not her own house, especially with her kids' birthdays both coming up in a couple of months. She picked up the box and carried it inside, setting it on the table. "You got a package!"

Mama Bear came around the corner, wiping her hands on a towel, likely from washing dishes in the kitchen. "Really? I haven't ordered anything that I know of."

Siren chuckled. "That you don't know of."

"Shut up, Siren," Mama Bear said as she walked over to the box.

Mama Bear slit the tape and opened the flap, peering in before her face went pale. She backed up from the table, yelling for Widow Maker. Tension swept through Siren's body as she approached the box. The smell of blood wafting toward her.

Still, she looked, and what she saw made her sick to her stomach. She stumbled back with her hand over her mouth. It was Lily, one of their newest members.

More accurately, her head.

Her hand still frozen on her mouth, Siren stared at the dark script on the box she hadn't noticed earlier; it was just one word that had her searching the limited Spanish she knew to trace back its meaning.

Sabemos. "We know."

Chapter 18
Chuckler

At nearly the same time, Chuckler walked out of the Jester clubhouse, his phone in his hand. His bike was finally ready, and he couldn't wait to take it out for a spin in the desert to see what it could do.

His boot kicked something in the doorway and Chuckler looked down, finding a box sitting there, waiting for someone to take it inside. Well damn, he couldn't just leave it there.

Picking it up, he turned and took it back inside, handing it to Ironsides. "Here."

Ironsides gave him a look. "What am I supposed to do with it?"

"I don't know," Chuckler said, with a shrug. "Open it?"

"You're a fucking asshole, you know that?" Ironsides remarked as he pulled open the flap.

Chuckler waited to see what was in the package, but then Ironsides's grin slid from his face and he nearly dropped the box.

"Shit, get Chains now."

"What is it?" Chuckler asked. It was then that the smell hit him, the smell of something dead.

Ironsides handed off the box to him, practically running to find Chains.

When he looked in the box, Chuckler nearly lost the sub he had eaten for lunch, staring at the severed pink-tipped hands barely covering a pair of women's breasts, the bloody edges of skin starting to turn black.

There was a note. Chuckler did all he could not to breathe in as he leaned forward into the box to make out the one word.

Sabemos. "We know."

Chapter 19
Rex

It was utter chaos, the room barely big enough to hold all the Jesters, much less the visiting Hell's Bitches in attendance. When I had seen what was in the box, I called Kris first.

Not just to see if she knew what the hell was going on, but also to hear her voice, to ensure she was alright. Two weeks ago, back around the time we got the clubs together, I'd deleted the tracker app that synched with the device attached to her bike, wanting to give her the line she deserved even if it meant I'd have to worry about her.

Though she was coming home to me every night.

But now, hell, I would be downloading the damn thing again after this threat.

With a nod to Chuckler, I rapped my knuckles on the table, the sound vibrating over the noise in the room. "I know you all have questions."

"Is one of us next on the list?"

"It had to be the cartel. Why the hell did you bring us into this shit, Chains?"

"We should back out now, pay them off, something."

I heard all of their concerns, feeling the weight of the club's worries on my own shoulders. When those body parts had shown up, I didn't know what to do. It wasn't one of ours, but either way, it was a message to all of us.

Don't cross the cartel.

Now, I didn't know what the hell to do.

"Where's her body?" one of the Hell's Bitches demanded. They all looked distraught over the loss. "We want to bury all of her, not just pieces."

I couldn't imagine what they were going through. "We will get her back."

"Who will?" one of my own called out. "This has nothing to do with us, nothing! You brought the damn cartel down on us and now we're gonna pay for it!"

"Meeting adjourned," I called out, seeing no other options. People were pissed, upset, confused, and grieving. I couldn't do this shit to them right now.

I had nothing to say.

Noting both Chuckler and Ironsides's looks of concern, I pushed away from the table and walked out of the room, down the hall to get a moment to take a deep breath.

"It's going to be okay," Kris's voice said next to me, her hand on my arm.

I turned to her, her red-rimmed eyes sucker-punching me in the gut. "Shit, Kris, I don't know what to do."

She wrapped her arms around my waist, and I pulled her in close, breathing in her scent.

"I don't either. I can't believe what they did to her. Why did they have to do that?"

"I don't know," I admitted, pressing a kiss into her hair. "But that will be the last one, I swear it." My club or not, I wasn't going to let innocent women being targeted like this. "No one will get to you."

She pulled back, wiping the tears away. "What did you say?"

I looked down at her, feeling the need to protect her at all costs tugging strongly on my heart. "No one is going to get you, Kris. I will protect you with my very life. You know that."

She stared at me for a moment before pulling out of my arms, seemingly pulling herself together. "I need to address my club."

"Me too," I said, blowing out a breath. I needed to make sure they had my back, though the horrors of getting the biker in pieces, even if she wasn't ours, shocked all of us. We all knew the cartel was brutal, but to take an innocent woman and chop her up like she wasn't shit, well, that was a side we hadn't seen up until now.

That and it made me want to know where Kris was at all times. She was my number one priority outside of the club, and I knew the cartel wouldn't hesitate to grab her to get back at me.

After all, they had taken one, what would stop them from taking another?

I didn't want to think about it. I didn't want to even entertain the idea of anyone being taken, much less Kris. "I'll give you fifteen minutes," I said, leaning close to her ear. "Then we are out of here."

She nodded and started off in the direction where her club gathered, while I stalked toward Ironsides and Chuckler who were deep in conversation.

"Keep the club quiet about this," I said. "I don't want mass hysteria."

Chuckler shook his head. "Dude, we are far beyond that. People are getting their families out of town as we speak. Everyone knows going against the cartel is a bad move."

I arched a brow. "You don't agree with my decision."

He gave me a look. "No, I agree, but it's still a bad move either way you look at it. Plus, knowing the cops are on their side, too? We don't stand a chance."

"Maybe not," Ironsides sighed. "But we made our choice." He glanced over in my direction. "With or without the Bitches backing, we made our choice."

I nodded, glad to hear he at least agreed with me. We had run for the cartel for too long, and now that we knew they were outwardly running innocent females across the border, well, the Jesters didn't agree with that. It could easily be one of our family members, our friends, our women. "I'm out."

Ironsides gave me a sideways glance as Kris came up. "Yeah, I bet. Don't worry. We won't burn down anything or get ourselves killed."

I shot him the finger before I turned to go, giving Kris a wicked grin. "You ready?"

She nodded, running a hand through her long hair. "Can we go to my place tonight? I feel like I need to be close to the club."

"Sure," I replied, not giving a fuck of where we went as long as we were together.

That was all that mattered.

***

Kris unlocked the door to her place and pushed it open, entering with a pizza in her hands. I followed close behind with the beer, kicking the door shut with my boot. The place hadn't really changed much since the last time I had been there. The same furniture adorned the rooms, and everything was a little bit messy just like I remembered.

This had been the furthest I'd gotten that night too, a few weeks after she moved out of my place. I'd been shocked when she opened the door to begin with, listening to me ramble on about all the reasons this was shit and why we should be together.

It hadn't worked. She had kicked me out for good, nearly shutting my damn hand in the door in the process.

But now, here was our second chance. We were meant to be together, we just had to make it work somehow.

"It's not much," she said, placing the pizza on the counter. "I'm not usually here anyway. I stay at the club more than anywhere."

"Me too," I admitted, setting the beer on the counter. But for far different reasons. The first year apart, the house reminded me of her, and I couldn't stand to be there unless I was drunk off my ass. I spent the night in whatever hold I could find, anywhere to avoid going back.

Then, after some time, the house started to feel like just a place to crash and I got used to the silence.

Kris unlaced her boots and kicked them off, shedding her vest in the process. "God, I am so tired."

I pulled off my jacket, placing it on the chair that butted against the bar top. "You want pizza here or in bed?"

She walked over, smoothing her hand over the front of my shirt. "Neither. I want you in my bed."

I framed her face with my hands, looking into her tired eyes. "Are you sure?" I wanted her so fucking bad, but I wasn't about to have sex with her if she was gonna fall out on me before we finished.

"Yes," she said, grabbing my hand and pulling me down the hall. "I need you, Rex."

Well, she didn't have to tell me twice. I allowed her to drag me down the hall and into a small bedroom where the bed dominated the space. "Shit. My closet is bigger than this," I answered as she spun me around.

"Shut up," Kris said, placing her finger on my lips. "Less talk, more touching."

I didn't know what her urgency was, but I wasn't going to argue with her right now.

Later, I would find out what was up with her.

Leaning down, I covered her mouth with mine, stroking my tongue against hers in a rhythm that I knew would make her sigh. I wanted to devour her, to make her forget about everything going on and focus on us.

And sigh she did. Her hands clawed at my shirt, sliding underneath it to touch my bare skin. Mine, meanwhile, worked on her jeans, pushing them over her hips and to the floor in a bid to get her naked.

Kris broke the kiss and I worked on her top, pulling it over her head and adding it to the pile on the floor. She stood in front of me, stark naked and my cock hardened uncomfortably against my jeans.

"Damn," I said softly, not touching her. "How did I ever get this damn lucky?"

She gave me a half smile, her eyes heated with desire. "I'm not sure. Maybe I have the wrong guy in my place tonight."

I growled. "I don't fucking think so. I am the only guy you will ever have in here from now on."

She looked as if she wanted to say something but closed the distance between us instead, pressing her lips against mine.

It was a long time before either of us came up for air.

**

Sometime close to midnight, I ground out a cigarette on the concrete and stared at the empty road leading to the apartment, feeling the press of the brick building through my jacket. Kris was nestled in her bed asleep, and while I wanted nothing more than to be curled up next to her, I couldn't.

I couldn't close my eyes without seeing the package we got or the fear in Kris's eyes when she told me about the matching one her club had received.

She was worried. And I didn't know what to fucking do to make that worry go away.

Blowing out a breath, I pulled out my cell phone, searching through the app store before I found the tracker app I had deleted just days ago. My thumb hovered over the install button and I hesitated, knowing she would kill me if she knew I was tracking her.

But the stakes were high now with the killing, and she was a target, one that Walker as well as the cartel would love to get their hands on. I couldn't take that chance. I couldn't let her just go do her thing without a safety net, without me knowing.

"Shit," I said under my breath as I pressed the install button, watching it start to download. She would understand. It had nothing to do with where she spent her time, but more so that I could find her at a moment's notice. We were partners in this.

There was no other reason.

Chapter 20
Kristina

I drew in a breath before I pulled the door open to the room that doubled as a meeting room and dining hall in the club. Every eye fell on me the second I stepped through the threshold. I had called an emergency meeting with my council, wanting to tell them first before they disseminated the information to the rest of the MC, knowing they would probably blow a gasket.

Not that we were much calmer. But I was trying to protect them. Surely they would see that.

Walking over to the table, I took my seat, rapping on the table with my knuckles, calling the meeting to order. "I know this was short notice, but I want to throw out the plan before you get wind from others."

"Oh shit," Mama Bear said, shaking her head. "This has to do with the Jesters, doesn't it?"

"Yes," I answered, deciding not to lie to them. They had to know it wasn't just us taking on the cartel. Rex and I had worked out strategic plans just a few hours before, albeit under the covers in my bed instead of an office.

It was my favorite way to do business now. I didn't know what made me want him to come to my place last night, but I was glad I'd brought him there. If we were going to make this work, he had to understand I had my own domain, and I wasn't just talking about the Bitches. I had moved on, made a life for myself, and I wanted him to be *part of* it… not just *it* like we were before.

"Go on," Siren said. "Lay it on us."

I looked at the women I trusted, the ones who were willing to lay down their lives for this club, for me as their president. "We will ride out in pairs from now on. One Bitch to one Jester at all times." Every time I closed my eyes, I saw them *all* carved up to pieces in a box, not just Lily. We were all targets now, and we had a better chance of survival if we banded together.

"What?" Robin 'Hair Trigger' Waters exploded, her eyes wide with shock. "You have got to be shitting me! I don't need no babysitter!"

"Yeah," Siren echoed. "We can handle our own shit."

"Oh yeah?" I said, arching a brow. "So, you're telling me if Lily had someone riding with her, that she still would have been targeted?"

"Listen," Mama Bear started, the only one who didn't look like she was ready to kill me in the room. "We are all upset about what happened to that poor girl, but that doesn't mean we need to overreact. This will make us look weak, like we're back to being club girl where most of us started. Didn't you form this club so we wouldn't be seen like that?"

"I did," I answered, gritting my teeth. "But I also want all of you to come home at night as well. The Jesters are willing to help. Why not use that muscle to our advantage?"

Mama Bear shook her head, pushing away from the table to stand. "I know we ain't got no say so in this, but I'm telling you right now, I won't be bullied around by no man who thinks he's above me. Been there, done that."

"I'm not asking for that to happen," I said, pissed off they were giving me so much lip. One of our own died violently and I was just trying to keep them all safe.

That was my job.

Siren shrugged as she pushed out of her chair. "Fine. Whatever. Just make sure they know we don't need their help in any other form."

My council walked out of the room, Mama Bear hanging back as I slumped back in my chair.

"Is it so wrong that I want to protect them all?"

She placed her hand on her hip. "Is that what you're doing, or are you just following orders again?"

I looked up at her, narrowing my gaze. "What do you mean?"

"I mean," she said with a huff. "All of a sudden we need *them* to protect us. We need *them* to help us stop the cartel. When did we decide we needed *them* anyway?"

"It's the cartel for God's sake," I tried. "How the hell are we going to beat the cartel by ourselves?"

Mama Bear pointed a finger at me. "Those aren't your words. The Widow Maker I know would have never gone begging for protection, no matter who was after us. You've let him start to think for you again and I don't like it."

"He's not thinking for me," I snapped, hating that some of her words might be right. "These are my thoughts."

"Whatever you say, Prez." Mama Bear let out a heavy sigh and headed to the door. "But don't forget how far you've come without him. You're better than that. We both know this."

She left and I put a hand over my face, wondering if maybe, just maybe, I had allowed Rex to talk me into this. Sure, we had discussed it, but... it had been his idea.

Not mine.

That was okay, right? I could agree to his ideas and still maintain my identity.

I could handle this. I could handle both my new life and Rex in it.

***

Three days later, I wasn't so sure we were going to survive this. I had listened to my club's grumbles for three whole days before they finally accepted their fate and agreed to ride out in pairs with the Jesters whenever on official club business. I knew Rex was getting as much flack about it as I was, though we didn't do much talking whenever we were alone.

No, it was more about satisfying each other, getting the frustration out of our systems, and desperately trying to hold onto what we had rekindled.

Well, when we weren't dead tired and falling asleep on each other.

Walker and his asshats in the police department made our lives a living hell, repossessing our bikes at the mere hint of a traffic or parking violation. I'd bailed out more bikes than I cared to count over the last few days.

But at least I didn't have raids going on like Rex had. For some reason, Walker thought it was funny to raid the clubhouse last night, pulling Rex from my bed and having him pissed off by the time he got back.

I understood his frustrations. We couldn't just kill the entire police department to get them off our backs, and any retaliation would only rain hell on the clubs and potentially put Leigh in danger as well.

No, we would have to think of something else, something other way to bring Walker to heel.

Heaving a sigh, I walked up the path to Rex's house, glad to be done for a few hours. The weight of the world was on my shoulders and with every phone call, every text, I became more and more concerned that maybe we'd made a mistake.

Maybe we shouldn't have taken on the cartel.

Walking inside, I found Rex seated at the kitchen table, a bottle of whiskey in front of him. "Wow," I said as I joined him. "And I thought I had a bad day."

He chuckled as I grabbed the bottle and took a swig, the fiery liquid burning a path straight to my stomach.

"Another two members got locked up today on some bullshit misdemeanor charge. At this rate, I'm not gonna have any cash left by the time I pay the lawyer to get them loose."

I sat the bottle back on the table, wiping my mouth with my hand. "This can't go on forever. He will move on."

"I hope," Rex sighed, picking up the bottle.

My cell buzzed in my pocket and I fished it out, frowning when I saw the unknown number. "This is Kris."

"Kris, thank God. I screwed up this time."

The frantic tone in Mama Bear's voice had me instantly concerned. "What is it? Is it the kids? Leigh?"

"No," she said in a rush. "I got busted with hot cargo. I'm calling you from jail."

Shit. She had been running a load today from California, dropping off guns in exchange for a large quantity of weed with one of the Jesters. I'd told her to wait until things settled down, but she had wanted a break from her kids and babysitting of our captive.

"How bad?"

She chuckled. "Well I'm in jail. That asshole Walker put me in the tank with the same Jester I just spent a shitload of time with. We don't have anything to say to each other."

"I'll send the lawyer," I said as Rex raised a brow.

"Alright, but I don't know what he can do for us this time," she said, blowing out a breath. "Just, make sure my kids are good, will you? I don't want them tangled up in this shit. Tell my mother to keep them for a few days."

"I will," I said.

She hung up. Placing the phone on the table, I bit my lip, willing myself not to scream in frustration. This could not be happening. This plan did not include Mama Bear getting arrested or looking at a potentially lengthy prison sentence.

"What is it?" Rex's voice grated through my thoughts.

I'd forgotten he was sitting there. I drew in a breath, staring at him. "Mama Bear is in jail with your guy. Walker busted them bringing the weed from California."

"Shit," Rex swore, pushing away from the table and standing. "I'll send my guy."

"I'm sending mine," I said, grabbing my cell and tapping out a text to the lawyer, then one to Mama Bear's mother about the kids. Of all the people who could have gotten busted with that amount of weed, Mama Bear was the one who had the most to lose. Walker would throw the book at her to prove a point and it made me sick to my stomach to think of a mother separated from her kids.

It was all my fault. "What have we done?"

Rex tucked his phone away as I placed mine on the table and rubbed at my throbbing temples.

"We are surviving Kris. They all knew the risk. Mama Bear knew what she could lose if she got busted."

His cold words sent the first sliver of doubt through my body. "It's our job to protect them."

He closed the distance between us, taking my arms in his hands. "Yes, it is. But they are adults, too. We didn't force them into this. Remember that."

That didn't make me feel better. I was responsible for my entire crew, good or bad, and putting them in this situation, with another club they didn't exactly trust, made me reevaluate my decisions.

Was it because Rex and I had gotten back together? It was easy when he was the 'enemy' and everything was so much clearer then.

Now, I didn't know where I stopped and he started.

"Hey," he said, tipping up my chin with his finger. "We will get through this. I can send a few guys to look out for Mama Bear's kids if that would make you feel better."

I looked into his eyes, seeing that possessive, protective streak flaring. No, no, we couldn't go down this road again, him always thinking he had to protect me from everything.

I was a fighter.

I was the president of my own damn club for God's sake. "No."

His nostrils flared and I knew he had been expecting me to fold.

"I mean, we will protect our own."

"Kris," he said, a hint of steel in his voice. "Let me help."

"You are," I said, grabbing his wrist and hauling him toward the bedroom. "By making me forget."

He didn't protest, but the first bricks had fallen on the invisible wall rising between us, the remnants of our past relationship gluing them into place.

Were we really meant to be together?

Crossing the threshold, I whirled him near the bed, desperately wanting to push all of this out of my brain for now. Mama Bear sitting in a cold cell, kids who wouldn't get a kiss from their mom tonight, Rex trying to protect me. It was too much. "Take off your damn clothes."

Rex arched a brow, a note of concern in his expression. "What's going on?"

"What?" I answered, pulling off my clothes. "I can't be in control for once?"

Chapter 21
Rex

Kris was losing it.

I could see it in her eyes, see the emotions swirling in them. Her mannerisms were jerky and weighed down, like she had the weight of the world on her shoulders and she was lashing out.

In a fucking bad way. "Are you sure you want to do this?"

She pulled off her jeans, exposing her long legs. "What? You don't want to fuck me?"

Oh, I did. I wanted to fuck her every second of the damn day. She was all I thought about.

But this Kris, I didn't know what to do with her. "Fine," I said, pulling off my boots and reaching for my shirt.

She watched from under hooded eyes as I stripped my clothes off, then placed my hands on my hips.

"What do you want me to do?"

"Get on the bed," she bit out.

I did as she asked, putting my hands behind my head. God, she was so emotional, so high-strung that I was actually scared.

Not that she was going to hurt me, but that she was going to fall apart.

Kris crawled on top of me and sank down on my hard cock, her body quivering around the intrusion. For a moment, she closed her eyes and I drank in the sight of her, my hands itching to touch her naked body. No foreplay, no warning, just raw sex between us.

I needed her just as much as she needed me.

When she started to move, I balled my fists into the pillow to keep from touching her. Kris wanted to be in control, and I was going to let her. We had played this game before, years ago, after her assault so that she would trust me in bed. Hell, I had given this woman a lot of leeway in the bedroom to keep that fear and anxiety out of her eyes.

Somewhere along the way, I'd fallen in love with her, and watching her now, I doubted I had ever stopped. Not even after six years and a bullet wound.

But when the first tear trickled down her cheek, I had to intervene, placing my hands on her hips to halt her movement. Hell, my damn cock shriveled up instantly. "Hey, stop. What is going on?"

She fell against me and I gathered her close, dislodging myself as her tears wet my bare chest. Kris was literally shaking in my arms, her sobs filling the air, and I did my best to comfort her, my hand rubbing her back lightly.

"Talk to me. Tell me what the fuck is going on."

"I failed," she said, her voice muffled by my chest. "I failed her."

"Oh, darling," I breathed, gripping her tighter. Kris was too soft to be put in this situation. Her heart wouldn't let her forget they were fucking adults and knew the risks. "It's not your fault."

She pulled back, the tears spiking her lashes. "But I am their president. I'm supposed to keep them safe! Mama Bear could be looking at a long stint in prison for this!"

"She could," I said, brushing her hair away from her face. "But we will do everything to keep her from going there. I swear it to you."

She sighed and laid her head against my chest, her hand resting near my now pounding heart.

"I don't know what to do, Rex."

Her voice nearly broke me. She sounded like the girl who had pushed her way through my door that night so long ago, the same girl who kept coming back no matter how much I pushed her away. I had tried everything, from telling her she wasn't a biker in a failed attempt at shutting her out. For her own sake.

But she hadn't given up and I didn't need her to start now. If Kris gave up, the rest of us were doomed.

"Hey," I finally told her, maneuvering the covers up over us. With her in my arms, I could protect her. "You'll be alright. I promise. I got you."

I couldn't lose her.

***

A few days later, I waited for Kris to come home, tapping my fingers along the table next to the bottle of beer. My mood was shit; I spent half the fucking day bouncing from one place to another to put out this fire and that. With the weed confiscated, we had to work out another deal, and I had driven back out there myself with Kris last night, our eyes open to any movement from Walker and his bunch of assholes.

Now my own damn bank account was short to cover the damn weed that was taken and we had a distrustful dealer in California who wondered if his product would remain safe during transport.

At least he hadn't shot my dick off for the loss.

The door opened and I straightened as Kris blew in, the haunted look in her eyes still there. Mama Bear was still in jail and every time our lawyers tried to bail her out, they raised the damn bail. Hell, she hadn't killed anyone and yet she was more expensive to spring than a murderer. I knew Kris visited her every day and was sending money to the kids, feeling like she was to blame for the woman being there.

No matter what I told her, she still believed it was her fault. "Hey."

"Hey," she responded, dropping into the chair. "You look like shit."

I felt like it. "I got something to show you."

She arched a brow, a hint of a grin on her face. "Didn't I see it twice this morning?"

I chuckled, reaching for my phone. "No, I'll show you that later. Maybe this will ease your mind a little."

She watched as I tapped on the screen, presenting the surveillance feeds I'd hooked up earlier. "See? You can watch the club from here, or anywhere for that matter. I have one on mine, too."

Kris frowned, peering at the screen. "You put a security camera up on my club?"

The way she said it made me want to squirm in my chair. She'd been so worried about the club over the last few days, I'd wanted to ease her mind when she was away from the physical building.

"It will give you a notification if Walker decides to do anything stupid."

Kris looked at me without even an ounce of excitement in her gaze. "You have this on your phone? What if you get busted and Walker gets his hands on this? He would have access to both our clubs!"

"I'm not planning on getting busted," I ground out. "By Walker or anyone."

Kris stood. "I can't believe this! Okay, so what if the cartel got a hold of your phone? You just put my club at risk, too, Rex. Without my permission."

I sat the phone on the table, looking up at her. "I think you are blowing this way out of proportion, Kris. I was just trying to help."

She glared at me. "You're trying to keep tabs on what we're doing, too, aren't you?"

"What the hell?" I answered, pissed she was trying to turn this shit into something it wasn't. "I'm trying to get you to fucking sleep at night without having to worry about your damn club!"

Kris let out a little laugh, shaking her head. "Oh my God. She was right."

"Who?" I barked out. "Who was right?"

"Nothing. Never mind. I'm going to bed."

I watched, dumbfounded, as Kris exited the room, wondering where in the hell this had gone south. I'd wanted to give her piece of mind, to take some of the weight off her shoulders. Somehow, she thought I was trying to control her and her club.

"Shit," I muttered, throwing boot across the room.

It didn't do much to calm me down, so I tried reasoning with myself. She just needed some time to see how this could benefit her, that was all. I wasn't trying to do anything but help.

But she saw my actions in some other light, some light I didn't understand. Picking up my beer, I drained it before throwing it in the trash and tucking my phone in my pocket. I would keep the feed for now, maybe have her warm up to the idea before showing it to her again. Surely she saw the benefit of it all.

Walking back to the bedroom, I stopped in the doorway, seeing her body curled up on one side of the bed instead of waiting for me to join her. The room was dark, but I could tell she wasn't naked under the comforter, the glow of a white shirt standing out in the dark.

Well hell, I was getting cock blocked too.

I stripped my clothes off and climbed in next to her, stretching my arms out under my head. Kris didn't move like she normally did, didn't curl up beside me or reach for me. I gave her a few minutes before turning over as well, staring at the damn wall across the room.

Whatever it was that had her pissed, I hoped it didn't last too long. I'd gotten used to having her wrapped around me every night, those little sounds she made when I hit the right spot. I didn't want this wall between us.

Hell, this was how it had started the last time.

We weren't going back.

I wasn't going to lose her again.

Chapter 22
Kristina

The crisp morning air filled my lungs as I tore down the highway, the morning dew not yet burned off by the rising sun. It was my favorite time of the day to ride. I preferred the lonely stretch of highway over any other stress relief these days.

And I had plenty of stress. My shoulders were tight, and I felt like I hadn't slept in days. Last night was the first night I hadn't slept with Rex or had his arms around me.

I hadn't known how much I'd grown used to his touch until last night.

Blowing out a breath, I kept my eyes on the road before me, wondering what I was going to do. Rex was acting like he used to, when he had overtaken my life and refused to let me make my own decisions.

Now I felt like I was in a time warp, where Rex was constantly trying to 'protect' me. The security cameras had nearly destroyed me, making me feel like I couldn't protect my own club. I was the president.

I'd protected my club for nearly five years, making decisions that would impact every member.

This decision to join the Jesters was quite possibly the worst one I had made to date, all because of Rex. There was no reason to lie. Any other president wouldn't have been able to talk me into doing something so rash, but Rex had.

Oh, how I hated to admit that he had gotten to me again! I wanted to hit him for reliving how I felt back then, like I had lost all handle on my life and my own decisions.

Rex hadn't intentionally meant for this to happen, I knew that. It was in his makeup, the need to protect me too overwhelming for him to overcome.

I didn't hate him. Oh no, that would be too easy. There were times, like last night, that I wished I could hate him.

Unfortunately, not a single bone in my body could hate Rex Harper, and for that, my heart hurt.

The sound of another engine caught my ears and I changed lanes, looking in my side mirror. Another biker gained on my tail, closing the space between us rapidly, and my heart caught in my throat. What if it was a member of the cartel, or Walker? I was out here by myself, with only one clip in my gun and no place to hide for miles.

Shit.

Shifting gears, I gunned it, the speedometer reaching ninety before I could blink. The wind tore at my hair and I knew at this speed, one good pothole in the road could be disastrous.

Glancing in my mirror again, I noted the biker kept up with me, the dot growing larger in my side mirror. Whoever it was, I was going to struggle to outrun them.

Making a split decision, I slowed my speed, reaching for my gun nestled in my side holster under my jacket. Thank God I'd started wearing it after Lily's death, afraid I might be the next target.

It might have saved my life this morning.

The bike's sounds grew louder, and I balanced the gun against my thigh, waiting for the right moment to aim and fire.

But when Rex's bike came into my view, I lowered the gun, inwardly breathing a sigh of relief. He motioned for me to pull over, which I did, killing the engine. Climbing off the bike, I leaned against it as Rex approached me, his eyes on me.

"How did you find me?" I asked, surprised. He was still asleep when I left.

He stopped short of reaching my bike. "You were riding like a bat out of hell. Have a death wish?"

He'd ignored my question. A trickle of fear slid down my spine when I saw the tick of his jaw, how he was now avoiding my eyes.

"What did you do?"

"What?"

I studied every flick of emotion in his face. "You know 'what.' How did you know I was out here?"

He shifted his stance. "Fine, I placed a tracker on your bike, alright? I wanted to know."

Oh God. He'd been tracking me. My throat closed off and I swallowed hard, feeling the box tightening around me. All of my concerns were true, then. Rex was the same guy I'd left all those years ago, wanting to control me and not let me, well, be me.

"When?" I asked, wanting to shoot him where he stood.

"The shop," he answered, eyeing me. "I did it for your own good."

"My own good?" I sputtered. "What part of this was to help me out, Rex?"

"Kris-" he started.

But I held up my hand. I wasn't going to deal with this right now. Getting tangled up with him again was a huge mistake. How could I have thought this would magically work out?

We weren't meant to be together. "Save it, you asshole."

"Kris, dammit," he said, grabbing my arm.

I whirled around and pushed at his chest, shaking off his touch. "There's nothing you can tell me that will make this better, Rex. I can't believe I thought you were taking me seriously."

"That's not what this is about," he ground out, pulling out his phone. "Here, I will delete it right now."

I snatched the phone out of his hand and threw it into the road, feeling some satisfaction when it broke into pieces. "No need. I just did it for you."

"That was childish."

I let out a laugh, feeling hollow inside. "Childish? You put a damn tracker on my bike! Tell me what that is this?"

"Protecting you," he replied.

I shook my head, walking back to my bike. "This is not protecting. This is invading my privacy." It like a shitty rerun to the past, when my life had morphed into his, and no matter what I said or did he'd shot it down.

And he'd always used the exact same reason for doing what he was doing right this minute.

Swinging my leg over the bike, I looked back at him. "Fuck you, Rex Harper."

His eyes narrowed, but I started the engine and pulled off, feeling my heart break all over again. This had been a mistake. I should have never trusted we could change, that he could change, or accepted that I had become my own person.

When it came down to it, I was still that scared girl who had looked up to him to save me.

I took the next exit to head back to the club, tears stinging my eyes that weren't just from the wind. Just when I thought things were going to go right for once, they had fallen apart so badly I didn't know if we could ever repair it this time around.

Another bike came into view in my side mirror and I set my jaw, giving the bike more gas and feeling it leap under my legs. Rex could run me down all he wanted to, but that didn't mean I would forgive him for this. He had gone too far, making his own judgment calls that had consequences for me and my club, without me knowing.

I wouldn't have been happy had he told me his plans ahead of time, but at least I would have known. This was like some big secret he'd kept from me on purpose. To think of how much he had followed my movements was both creepy and disheartening.

I took the next turn faster than I intended, feeling the bike shift and nearly upend me at the same time. For a split second my heart stopped as I wrestled with the handling of the bike, getting it straight and not laying it down. I was being stupid going this fast, but I wanted nothing more than to lose Rex off my ass.

I didn't want to talk right now.

Slowing down, I turned down the road to the club, the smell of smoke in the air.

No, it can't be.

Forgetting all about my speed or my safety, I took the next two turns like the hounds of hell snipped at my heels, my heart in my throat as the house came into view.

My worst fear was confirmed.

The Hell's Bitches club house was on fire.

Chapter 23
Rex

Kris was off her bike before I could even stop mine, running toward the burning building with her long hair streaming behind her. I climbed off my bike, both afraid for her and for anyone else who could be in the burning structure.

I had fucked things up with Kris. There was no doubt about it. That look in her eyes, the way she had gone off over the tracker. Things had gone to shit.

Pushing those thoughts out of my mind, I ran over to the building, trying to find Kris amongst the chaos. There were women everywhere, along with the firefighters who had just arrived on scene. People sobbed in the grass, some screaming out for others still inside.

I pushed my way through the gathering crowd, seeing Kris at the doorway, flames all around her.

"Kris!" I shouted, running toward her. The building could fall on her and the damn woman was right in the middle of it.

She looked up a half a second before I grabbed her, pulling her out of harm's way with her kicking and screaming the whole time.

"You are going to get yourself killed!"

She struggled in my arms, sobbing. "Let me go! My girls are in there!"

I held her against my chest, locking her against me. There was no way in hell I was going to let her run back into that burning building. She could be pissed at me all she wanted to, but I was holding my damn life in my hands.

I wasn't going to let her go like that.

The roof crashed in with a shower of sparks and flames, and Kris let out a mournful sound, tearing my damn heart in two. She was in pain and I was clueless as to how to help.

How to make it go away.

"They are in there!" she cried out, struggling against my hold. "Dammit Rex, let me go!"

"No," I bit out, letting my feelings come out in that one word. "I won't lose you."

"You already have," she sobbed, slumping against my chest, her tears falling onto my arm.

I steeled myself against the pain that sliced through my chest.

But this just proved a point, this moment right here. Kris was willing to throw herself into that fire to save her other member's lives and didn't give a shit about her own, or how it would impact anyone else.

If I wasn't holding her, I would have already lost her.

***

Thirty minutes later, the fire marshal gave the all clear and Kris, who had been standing off by herself, started toward the building. I followed her, my jaw set as I watched her step inside the half-burned structure. The front part of the building was gone, reduced to ash and charred wood. The back half of the building was made of cement blocks, and besides some charring on the blocks themselves, along with water damage, it was largely intact.

But the house was the least of my concerns. The three blue tarps amongst the wreckage stood out against the blackened mess, three club members who hadn't made it out alive. Swallowing hard, I stood near the building, my eyes on Kris. The two remaining members of her council, Siren and Hair Trigger, walked beside her, keeling down near each tarp.

That could have been Kris. The thought was a sucker-punch to my gut as I thought about her lying there under those tarps. I was unable to protect her in her own club. She had no idea what that did to a man, to me. What if I hadn't followed her this morning? What if she had been here when whoever was who had set fire to the place?

I couldn't deal with it.

Kris stood and looked around at the members who still stood there glassy-eyed, waiting for her next word. "Go home to your families. Let them know you are safe. This isn't going to destroy us."

There were murmurs, but the crowd did as she asked. Kris looked down at the tarps and took a shuddering breath.

I gave her a moment before I approached her, and reached out to touch her arm. "Kris."

She shook off my touch, her eyes full of loss. "Don't. Just don't."

I ground my teeth together. "Let me take you home. I got a few guys coming to help clean up."

"Oh my God," she said, shaking her head. "You don't ever learn, do you? I don't need your help, Rex."

I took a step closer. "You could have died today if it wasn't for me. Face it, you need me, Kris."

Kris took a step back, putting some space between us. "I've lived five years without you, Rex, and I've done just fine."

"Oh really?" I laughed. "Your fucking club is in turmoil Kris. Your clubhouse is ash. If this is your definition of fine, then you are wrong."

Kris flinched as if I'd struck her and I instantly regretted my words. None of this was her fault. All of this was happening because we turned against the cartel.

"You have no idea what it is like to be powerless," she said in a soft voice. "To have nothing in your grasp."

I knew what she was talking about. I had seen her at her worst. "You don't know what it's like for me to stand aside and watch you refuse my help, Kris. Hell, I feel powerless watching you struggle."

She bit her lip. "I haven't struggled, Rex. Can't you see what I've done without you in my life? Can't you see that I am my own person?"

"Is that what you're trying to prove?" I said. "And if it hadn't been for me, you would be dead right now, just like those members under the tarps there."

She let out a harsh laugh. "Oh, I see. I can't even protect myself or my club in your eyes, can I?"

"You won't protect your club," I shot back. "I've tried to help, but for some damn reason, you won't accept it."

"I won't accept it," she countered, "because I don't need your fucking help, Rex. I don't need your club and I don't need you."

"Yes you do!" The words tumbled out of my mouth before I could stop myself. "You are nothing but a scared club girl playing president, who has no idea what the hell she's doing!"

Her expression changed and before I knew it, she had her gun in her hand. "Get the hell off my property."

I arched a brow. "What? You'll shoot me again?"

"I will if I have to," she answered, her jaw set. "I don't want to see you or your club around here, Rex, or I will be forced to protect my own."

Well this had just gone to shit. "I'm not your enemy, Kris."

"Then stop acting like one." She motioned with her gun. "Go, before I shoot you. I've done it before."

That she had. I hesitated, knowing I'd crossed some line with her today, starting with the tracker and ending with insulting her. How had this gotten to this point?

"What? You don't think I will?" Kris continued, pissed off I hadn't started to leave. "Fine, have it your way."

The gun went off, the bullet pinging in the dirt at my feet, and I stared hard at her, surprised she had fired the weapon. Her jaw set, her eyes flashing in anger, she held the gun up to my face.

"The next one will be between your eyes, Rex. Your choice."

"Fine," I said, seeing I wouldn't be able to reason with her now. "But this isn't over between us, Kris."

"It is," she answered. "I never want to see you again."

I didn't turn back, making my way to my bike, feeling her eyes on me the entire way. So, she wanted to play it like this. I could do that, but I wouldn't be bossed around by her for long. Kris and her club were in serious danger and they couldn't handle the cartel and Walker without help. Somewhere deep down, I knew Kris knew that too, but her grief was too much right now.

So, I gave her what she wanted.

I left.

Chapter 24
Kristina

I watched as Rex sped away, feeling my heart break into a thousand pieces as he did. I was hurt, devastated, angry, and at a loss of what to do next. My club was burned to the ground, three more of my members dead, and I had forced Rex out of my life.

Taking in a shaky breath, I nodded to the medical examiner to allow them to start removing the bodies from the clubhouse, before walking down the half burned-out hall to my office, which reeked of smoke and had puddles of water all over the place from the fire hoses. We hadn't lost the entire club, which was a good thing, but three lives had been taken from us today.

Three innocent lives.

Tears crowded my eyes and I sat down behind my desk, ignoring the water that seeped into my jeans from the wet chair. Rex's harsh words had sliced my heart in two. He had so little faith in what I could do, what I had done without him in my life.

But I wasn't the scared girl he thought I still was. I was this club's president, responsible of our next move. Everyone was waiting for me to make the call of whether we continued our pursuit of the cartel or slink back into the shadows.

I couldn't allow that to happen. We had worked too hard taking down those shipments for us to back out now.

But our time with the Jesters was in jeopardy of ending. How would I face Rex after this day?

Slumping in my chair, I let the tears fall, tired of holding them back. Though his words had been hateful, I knew he was just trying to protect me the only way he knew how. It would have been easy to fall back against him, let him take charge and take away the pain that threatened to rip me in two. Rex was like that, the man who could make everything go away and shelter me from the hurt.

But the moment I let him do that, I would lose everything I had worked so hard for over the last five years. There were glimmers of the old me starting to bleed through and I hated it. I didn't want to turn back into that woman who waited in the wings, waiting for someone to make her decisions for her.

I would have to decide where our next steps were, assuming my club still wanted me making the decisions. I had screwed up this time, pulling us into a war we might not survive. I had let myself be weak, and allowing Rex to influence some of my decisions.

Mama Bear had been right. Rex was making commands through me.

Wiping my face, I thought about the conversation I would have to relay to my second in command. I hadn't gone to see her in two days, pissed off that she was even there to begin with and afraid to face the possibility that I wouldn't be able to get her back to her kids in the end. Walker was pressing for federal charges, and if that happened, she would go to prison for quite some time.

It was all my fault.

Maybe Rex was right instead. I was just a scared club girl still, winging it as I went along.

"Widow Maker? You shouldn't be in here."

I looked up to see Siren in the doorway, her eyes red-rimmed and puffy. "Why?"

"The smoke," she said. "It's not good to be breathing in right now."

I shuffled some of the papers on my desk, flinging them in the trash in disgust. "Well just because the club is gone doesn't mean the work stops." I needed something to keep my mind occupied.

"I did an ammo check," she said after a moment. "We are lucky they didn't take one of the sheds. Would have been fireworks for sure."

I nodded, standing. "Thank God for little things, I guess. I thought I told you to go home."

"You did," she responded as I threw another stack of water logged papers in the trash. "I saw what happened and I'm sorry. He's wrong, you know. You're stronger than any of us."

My heart squeezed painfully in my chest. "I'll leave in five minutes, okay?"

"Okay," Siren said.

I waited for her footsteps to echo down the hall before I looked up, glad to see the doorway empty. I didn't need her to tell me I was strong. I knew I was strong.

But I didn't know how strong I was with my back against the wall. Rex had told me once that I could be as strong as I would let myself be, which was funny seeing as he always wanted to protect me.

I flung the rest of the contents from the desk to the floor with my hand, satisfied at the sound ricocheting off the walls. We would rebuild the club, make it stronger than ever. I had no qualms about staying the course now, I wouldn't tuck my tail between my legs and run.

I wanted to take down the cartel.

A glinted piece of metal caught my eye and I stooped down, picking it up with some surprise. It was a metal rose, one I had forgotten was on my desk. Lord, how had I not noticed it for the last five years? The rose was one of the first gifts Rex had given me, and while I'd left everything else at the house when I left, I'd taken the tiny rose with me, leaving it on my desk when I started up the club as a reminder of everything I'd been through.

Now it brought nothing but sadness.

Reaching out with my finger, I touched the small petals, a small smile drifting across my face. It was the first time Rex had shown his soft side to me, the gruff biker surprising me when I thought I couldn't be surprised by anything else in my life.

***

I drew in a breath and knocked on the door, my heart beating wildly in my chest. Tonight was going to be the night. I was going to give myself to Rex Harper.

There was still a piece of me that was scared to open myself up to anyone again, especially in a sexual nature, but the last month had turned into something completely unexpected for me. Maybe it was the fact that every time I showed up at his doorstep, he let me in, ignoring the hell out of me for the most part, but not kicking me out.

Or maybe it was because I couldn't stop thinking about him, and how it would feel to have sex with Rex, the man who had saved me when he could have easily turned his back on me.

I knew the risks, having hashed them out in my head more than once over the last week or so. He could easily have me and move on, getting what he wanted, or well, what I thought he wanted anyway. There had been nothing more than a casual brush of our arms when we rode his bike together, and when he took me to the bar just two nights ago, I'd clung to him, taking on the mannerisms of the other women in the room and claiming him as mine.

And now I wanted him to really *be mine. I wasn't doing this to erase what James had done to me.*

I wanted to live again.

The door opened and Rex stood there like he always did, his arms crossed over his bare chest. My mouth went dry as I took in his strong form, the way a sprinkling of dark hair covered his chest that I wanted to touch.

Not to mention what might be under those jeans of his.

"Are you just gonna stare at me or did you want to come in?"

I swallowed hard, bringing my gaze back to his and saw the grin on his face. I wanted to say something witty, something that would make him see I was much more than that girl he rescued, but my mind was completely blank. "I want to come in."

He arched a brow, but to my relief, stepped aside to let me in. "You don't give up, do you?"

I shrugged out of my coat, smiling when I heard his sharp intake as he took in my attire. I had pulled out a low-cut, short dress that showed off my body, far more risqué than anything he had ever seen me in.

This felt right.

"What are you doing, Kris?" he asked as I turned, allowing him to see the front of the dress.

"I'm trying to tell you that I want you," I said, my voice shaking.

Rex shook his head. "You don't want me. You're looking for someone to take the pain away and I'm not that fucking man."

I closed the distance between us, standing before him, but not touching him.

Yet. "I've thought about this and you are what I want."

He stared at me for a minute. "You don't belong here, Kris."

It was then I knew I had won. "Shut the door, Rex."

***

I shook out of the memory, feeling the excitement still fluttering in my chest I'd felt that night, that special night that had tied us together. His touch had been gentler than I could have imagined as his mouth traced every inch of my body.

And in that morning light, this rose had been on the pillow beside me, a promise of something more between us.

Sighing, I tucked the rose in my vest pocket, unable to leave it. That had been a time when everything was right with the world and we had each other.

But now, everything was so confusing. We couldn't have each other even if we wanted to, not with the way we had left it. I couldn't trust him to let me be the woman I had become, and Rex couldn't let go of his overprotective nature.

Not matter how much we wanted to be together, it wasn't in the cards for us.

I didn't know how that made me feel.

Taking one last sweep of the office, I walked out, my body drained. There were a thousand things I needed to do, things to figure out for the future of the club and me being president.

But as I cataloged it all in my head, there was really only one thing I wanted to do right now, and it had nothing to do with the club.

No, all I wanted to do was chase Rex down and have him put his strong arms around me, tell me everything would be alright. The hardest thing I'd done was send him away today, when my life was falling apart.

He was gone and I didn't know if we could ever repair the damage that had been done, but it didn't make me stop loving him. It didn't make me shut off the feelings, shut off the need, and close him out of my life forever.

It only made me want to find him even more.

Blowing out a breath, I crossed over the threshold to the burned structure, seeing that the bodies were gone.

It was time to rebuild.

Chapter 25
Rex

Whoever invented liquor, more specifically tequila, should win a fucking medal.

I downed another shot, no longer feeling the burn in the pit of my stomach. I didn't know if it had anything to do with the six other empty shot glasses that lined the bar top, or if I had gone numb to the effect, but I didn't care.

It was good to feel no pain.

Motioning for another, I ran a hand over my beard, a frown on my face. After I had left the Hell's Bitches clubhouse, I'd tried to see if I could get any notion of who had burned their place down, roughing up a few of the bottom feeders for information because it felt good to put my fist into someone else's face.

Now I didn't even feel the burn of my busted knuckles.

"Man, oh man. Chains getting wasted? What's the occasion?"

I picked up the next shot, holding it steady as Ironsides sat next to me with a grin on his face.

"Do I need a reason?"

He shrugged. "Usually, no. But I can probably guess why you're drinking like this."

I knew he could. He knew me better than anyone. Well, except Kris. "Did you get anything done?"

"Yeah," Ironsides replied.

I noted that soot covered his hands. The smoke smell clung to his clothing and filled my nostrils.

"We cleaned out the debris. The guards didn't put up much of a fight and she didn't show up to stop us. I think they're in shock."

I was in shock, but I wasn't about to say it out loud. "Thanks."

"No problem," he sighed. I passed the shot off to him and he downed it, setting the glass back on the wood. "I bet it was Walker trying to scare them again."

I didn't know it, but I was nearly out of my mind with worry for Kris. She had been pissed, beyond pissed today, and I didn't know if I could fix it.

If either of us was strong enough to fix it.

"So," Ironsides continued while the bartender poured him another shot. "Care to tell me what happened?"

I rolled my shoulders uncomfortably. Damn it was stupid to think I could drink her away. It hadn't worked then, and it sure as hell wasn't going to work now. "She hates me."

He chuckled. "We already knew that, though. I thought you had changed her mind about her feelings for you."

"I really did it now," I said, thinking of the way she had looked at me when I had told her she wasn't strong enough to be president of her own damn club. That wasn't the truth. Hell, Kris was the strongest person I knew, stronger than me most of the time.

And what she had been through over this last month? A weaker woman would have tucked tail and ran from the danger, given up when she couldn't find the glimmer of hope.

Kris had raided our shipments on her own, turned my club on its ear about what we were going to do for our future, and moved me from wanting her to loving her again.

Not that I'd ever stopped loving her.

"There it is," Ironsides broke through my thoughts. "That's the look of a man in love. Tell me I'm wrong."

"That's not the problem," I ground out. I loved her too damn much. "I told her she shouldn't be president."

"Shit," he breathed, letting out a low whistle. "Why the hell would you do that? She's been carrying that club for five years, man."

"Hell, I don't know," I admitted, feeling like the lowest asshole on the planet. "I'm scared I'm gonna lose her."

"Well, you are doing a fine job of pushing her away." He picked up the next shot. "Kris has changed. You might as well get used to that fact."

Oh, I knew that. She seemed sure of herself, no longer hiding in the corner but right in front, begging for someone to pick her. She had gone from a woman scared of her own damn shadow to someone, well, someone I admired.

"Let me ask you something," Ironsides continued. "Five years from now, could you be content with sitting back and watching her grow that club into something to be rivaled? What if I started sniffing around her? Could you watch that?"

I snarled at him. "Keep your nose far away from her."

"I'm not gonna hit on her," he groused, shaking his head. "Man, you have it bad. It was just a damn question."

She was making me crazy. "Sorry."

"No offense taken." My best friend shrugged. "But I think you should save your apologies for Kris. Go, tell her you're sorry. Take her some damn flowers if you need to."

I chuckled. "She doesn't want flowers."

"Then take her a bike, but don't let this one get away this time. As much as I hate to admit it, you two belong together and I don't want to have to deal with your sulking ass any longer than necessary."

I looked over at him. "You think you can deal with us both again?"

He shook his head. "Listen, they just want to have their power, too, for us to step aside every once and awhile. Treat them like an equal and they will love you for it."

Arching a brow, I looked at the man who had spent years by my side. "How did you become such an expert in these women?"

He looked away, sliding off the stool. "Better you don't know. My turn to take watch. Don't fall off the damn stool. I don't want to have to pick your ass off the floor again."

I watched as he walked away, wondering what was up with Ironsides. It seemed I had been so wrapped around Kris that I had missed something important in his life, something I would have to figure out later.

But right now, he was right. I needed to grovel in front of her, find out how we could make this work between us. I didn't like this separation between us, this wall that we were both trying to push against. I wanted her in my bed, in my house, or wherever she wanted to be.

As long as it was with me.

Blowing out a breath, I pushed away the last shot, standing wobbly legs. I'd had too many. I didn't like having my head fuzzy, preferring to keep my wits about me at all times.

Walking back to my office, I sat down at my desk and kicked my feet up. I would catch some sleep to get rid of the alcohol in my system and then plot my return into Kris's life.

That and figure out how we would both get out of this shit with Walker and the cartel. I wanted to be free and clear of both the crooked sheriff and of the cartel so we could live in some sort of peace.

Until we did that, there would always be that fear of what Kris was involved in, and I was sure she felt the same way about me. That fear tore us apart the first go around and I didn't want to make that mistake again.

I leaned back in my chair, suddenly stone-cold sober. I didn't want to go home tonight to an empty house, knowing Kris wouldn't be there waiting on me. I didn't want to sit in that house, on that bed, and have only her memory.

I had to get her back.

I just had to.

Chapter 26
Kristina

I drew in a breath, tasting the acrid smoke in the air on my tongue. I knew by the nervous glances that my council and my club members were surprised I had called a meeting here, where we lost three members, and where it looked like our club ended in ashes.

But that was exactly why I had called a meeting here, on this spot where part of our club was missing. "I've called you all here tonight because I wanted to apologize for this."

I raised my arm and pointed to the burned-out shell that had been our great room. "I caused this. I caused the deaths of four of our sisters in arms and I will never, ever forgive myself for that."

My throat closed with emotion, but I forced it down, hating what I had to do. I loved this club with every fiber of my being, but because of my stupidity, I had nearly gotten them all killed.

I wasn't going to make that mistake again.

I forced myself to reach up and rip off the patch label on my vest, swallowing hard as I laid it down on the table before me. "I'm resigning as president of Hell's Bitches."

Murmurs rose up as I stepped back and attempted to hold myself together for the sake of the club. The decision had been a difficult one to come to, but after today, after I lost Rex, I realized that maybe he was right in all this.

Maybe I was just a scared little girl pretending to be something I could never be.

"This is bullshit."

Jessie stepped forward, staring hard at all of us. "I don't know about the rest of you, but Widow Maker here has done everything she can for this club. So, what we made an enemy of the cartel? We were gonna do that anyway with what we were doing with the Jesters." She turned to me. "None of this is your fault."

"She's right," Siren echoed, her eyes on me. "With Mama Bear indisposed, I am the senior ranking member of your council and I refuse to accept your resignation."

Hair Trigger stood up next to her, her hands on her hips. "I agree. We don't want your resignation, Widow Maker. You *are* this damn club and we didn't sign up to drink tea and talk about the weather. We knew the risks, all of us."

"This is family," Siren added, picking up my patch. "And you are the head of it."

I swallowed hard as I took the patch from her, staring at the sea of faces I knew better than my own. I had failed them. I had dragged them down a path I thought was the best idea at the time and it had backfired in my face.

Yet they still wanted to keep me as their leader. "I don't know what to say."

"Say you are gonna put that damn patch back on your vest," Siren replied, laying a hand on my shoulder. "And you aren't gonna give up."

I gave her a grateful smile, doing all that I could to not break down in tears. "Then that's what I will do."

"Good," Jessie said, giving me a nod as I slapped the patch back onto its Velcro bed.

They were right, damn them. I would be giving up on the very thing that had kept me going all these years, during the tough times that had threatened to take me under.

Hair Trigger came over and gave me a hug, something completely out of character for her. Stunned, I returned it, feeling a stray tear slip down my cheek. These women, they were my family.

"We will get through this," she said. "You might have gotten us in this shit, but I have no doubt that you are gonna get us out of it."

Before I could say anything, she moved on and the next club member was hugging me, until the entire club had done the same. I was speechless. While we were close, they'd never shown this sort of affection toward me.

After the last woman had stepped past me, I turned to face my club. "We will fight. We will rebuild, and we will make sure no one steps on Hell's Bitches again."

"Hell yeah," Hair Trigger said, a smirk on her face. "So, what's the plan, boss?"

"First," I started, motioning for Jessie to join me, "we make this one a real Hell's Bitch."

Cheers went up as Jessie turned to face me, a crooked smile on her face.

"Prospect," I said, laying a hand on her shoulder. "Do you promise to always protect your sisters at all costs, even with your life?"

"I do," she answered, her eyes shining.

I gave her a nod. "You have proved your self-worth to this club in more than one way. You have passed the test and I can see no reason to not make you an official member. Do I have an 'Aye' from the club?"

"Aye!" they all chorused together, their voices ringing out in unison.

I gave her a grin. "The 'Ayes' have it. Welcome to the club, Rivet."

"Rivet?" she asked.

"For holding us together during a difficult time," I said, my words heartfelt. Had she not spoken up, I would not be in a place to do this.

Rivet gave me a sharp nod before turning toward the rest of the group, who were ready with their congratulations. My cell buzzed in my back pocket and I stepped away, feeling my heart beating fast in my chest. It had to be Rex. I didn't know what to do, what I would say to him. Actually, I was scared to even hear his voice. What had transpired between us was something I didn't know if we could fix or not.

I wanted to fix it. I hated the words we'd said, the way we had left each other earlier. I loved Rex more than anything, more than my club or the patch on my vest, and while I knew he struggled with his protective nature, he hadn't done anything to hurt me.

But there would be changes if we did reconcile. He would have to learn to give me some space and trust I knew what the hell I was doing.

Reaching for my phone, I held it up to my ear. "Hey, I'm here."

"Good," a familiar voice said on the other side. "Because what I have to say, you are going to want to listen, Widow Maker."

"Walker," I said. "What the hell could you tell me that I would actually want to hear?"

He chuckled. "Well for starters, these kids would go for a pretty price in the Mexican market."

The blood drained from my face. I didn't need to ask who he had. I could feel it in my heart. "Don't you fucking hurt them."

"I don't plan to," he answered. "If you do what I say and the way I say it."

"I'm listening," I said, my eyes on my club.

"You will come to the address I text to you," Walker replied. "Unarmed and alone. The first hint of you bringing company, and I will kill the kids after I kill my pretty little ex here."

Shit. He had Leigh, too. The kids were bad enough, but knowing the history between Walker and Leigh, I knew she was in grave danger. "You don't have to harm any of them. I will come wherever you want me to."

"I knew you would see it my way," he said. "You got one hour, Widow Maker, before I start shooting off fingers."

I lowered the phone as Siren approached me, her expression full of concern. "What? What is it?"

"Walker has the kids and Leigh," I let out. I might be willing to follow his orders, but I sure as hell wouldn't keep them in the dark.

"That bastard," Siren scowled. "What do you want us to do?"

"I have to go by myself, his demand," I said. "But I need for you to contact Chuckler or Ironsides now."

Siren clenched her jaw, her eye flashing with annoyance at having to reach out to the Jesters.

"Listen," I continued, laying a hand on her shoulder. "We need help. I will call Chains, but I need for you to make amends with them. It's for the kids."

Siren let out a slow breath. "Okay, you're right. I will call them now, but you know you can't go there by yourself."

I started to move away, giving her a wry grin. "I don't plan to." I wanted to have a backup plan, if nothing more than to keep my club safe, but the moment I dialed up Rex, he would come.

There was no doubt in my mind.

Halfway to my bike, I turned back to Siren. "You are in charge. If something happens, until Mama Bear is free, the club is in your hand."

"Kris-" she started, looking uncertain.

I gave her a wink. "I will send you the address. Just make sure you call them."

"I will," she called out.

I approached my bike, my cell in my hand. I waited until Siren turned back toward the clubhouse before I dialed Rex's number, my heart hammering against my chest. I wanted to talk to him.

Just not in this way.

"Kris."

The relief in his voice nearly tore me in two. "Rex, I- Walker called me. He's got the kids and Leigh."

"Shit," he answered. "What does he want?"

"Me," I replied as I swung my leg over my bike. "I'm going there now."

"No you're not," he started. "You can't go in there by yourself. Wait, I'll meet you."

"It has to be me, and me alone," I said. "But I need you to track me."

"Dammit, Kris."

"Text me when you're close," I forced out, a light quiver in my voice. "I love you."

I didn't wait for him to answer, hanging up before he could unleash his wrath on me. I could only imagine how pissed he was now, but it was the best I could do.

Rex would come for me. There was no doubt about that.

***

I arrived at the location with fifteen minutes to spare, noting the desolate house at the end of a long, dirt driveway. Why Brad had chosen this location was beyond me, but if I had any inclination of freeing the hostages or running myself, it was a long shot now. We would be like target practice running across the barren land that was without a tree for hundreds of yards.

I pulled my bike close to the house, reaching down to check my ankle holster before anyone walked outside. I wasn't stupid. I might not get a chance to use it, but I wasn't about to walk in there unarmed.

Patting my back pocket, I felt the comforting rectangle of my cell phone, hoping and praying the service was still good way out here. If it wasn't, I was all alone, and the outcome was likely going to suck for me.

Two Hispanic men walked out onto the porch, eyeing me with interest. They both wore the colors of Los Aztecas wrapped around their heads, the butt of their handguns visible from their waistbands.

It seemed I wasn't just dealing with Walker. Holding up my hands, I gave them a saucy smile. "Relax, boys. I was invited."

One motioned with his hand, the other with his gun. "The boss wants to see you."

"Perra," the other spat out, his eyes narrowing as I climbed the steps onto the porch.

I shot him the middle finger and breezed past, hearing his string of curses as I did so. I wasn't going to show them I was scared to death about being there.

I was the president of Hell's Bitches and I would be 'til they put a bullet in my head.

I just hoped Rex would get here before then.

The interior of the house was dark and musty smelling, devoid of furniture but full of men. I stopped just short of the doorway, trying to hide my panic when I saw the kids in the corner, bound and gagged. Leigh stood near Walker who held her by the waist with a gun pressed to her forehead. Surprisingly, she looked rather calm about it despite the tears streaking down her face.

"Well, well, you did show up."

I put on a grin. "Did you think I wouldn't? How could anyone resist this invitation?"

A man stepped out of the shadows and I recognized him instantly, the tattoo on his neck making him far too easy to spot. "Cesar, this is a surprise. I didn't know you liked crooked cops."

Cesar rubbed his hands together. "I like anyone who can make me money, querida. You know that." His eyes swept over my body, lingering for a second too long on my breasts. "No wonder they talk about you."

"Yeah, about how she is a pain in my ass," Walker tightened his hold on Leigh and yanked her head towards him. "Because of you, I still have this bitch to deal with. I ought to shoot you where you stand for the trouble you caused me."

"No, no," Cesar interrupted, holding up his hand. "This woman is a smart one, aren't you?"

"I like to say I am," I answered, glancing at the kids. They looked unharmed for the most part, and while I needed to get all three of them out of here alive, the kids were my main priority.

I imagined Leigh wouldn't say anything different.

"You are, you are," Cesar said, touching the gun in his waistband. "And you want those brats over there, don't you, Widow Maker?"

"I do," I said, turning my gaze on him. "What do I need to do to get them?"

"Die," Walker said, turning his gun on me. "That would solve all of my damn problems."

"Stop being so dramatic," Cesar demanded, looking at his partner. "Before I shoot you myself."

Walker grumbled but lowered the gun, not bothering to put it against Leigh's head this time. I silently calculated my odds in my own head, the outcome still not looking very good for me.

Shit, what was I going to do?

Just then, my cellphone buzzed in my pocket and I smiled, unable to help it. Rex was close. He was about to save the damn day and I couldn't wait for him to do so.

But first, I had to do some distracting of my own. "Again, before we were rudely interrupted, what do I need to do to get those kids from you, Cesar?" I asked, dropping my voice to a sultry level.

He grinned, just like I knew he would, and pulled out his gun, motioning me to close the gap between us.

I took my time, walking toward him without an ounce of fear. Whatever he had planned for me, it wasn't going to last long.

He pointed to the floor and I dropped to my knees, looking up at him. "What do you want me to do for you?"

He pressed the steel barrel of the gun to my temple as his other hand went to the front of his pants. "You're going to beg my forgiveness for all the shit you have put me through while sucking my cock."

The rest of the room snickered but I ignored them, trying to make myself look like an eager participant so Cesar wouldn't get an itchy trigger finger with this gun pressed up against my head. He succeeded in pulling out his cock with one hand, the thing flopping out like an ugly, limp noodle.

Rex couldn't get here soon enough.

Chapter 27
Rex

I looked through the scope of my gun, my brain firing off warnings left and right. If I missed my target, Kris would end up dead.

If I hit my target, she might still wind up dead.

Sweat trickled down my forehead as I watched the rest of the Jesters and Bitches surround the house, already silently taking out the few lookouts posted there. It seemed everyone was focused on Kris on her knees, with her hand on Cesar's dick, and his gun pressed against her head.

I wanted to shoot his cock off.

Damn, she had put me through some shit in the last hour or so. First her phone call, and now, the gun to her head.

I was gonna need a week to recuperate after this one.

With Kris.

In our bed.

The signal went up and I pulled the trigger, watching through the scope as the bullet struck Brad Walker right between the eyes. He did a slow fall to the floor and Cesar looked up in shock, but I was already on the move, leaving the sniper rifle in favor of my hand gun.

Gunfire erupted on the inside as I approached the house and I wasted no time dropping another Azteca as I barreled through the door.

Shit. There was no place to hide in there. The room was empty with the exception of strewn bodies on the wooden floor.

"Oh God, oh God!"

Leigh was on her knees, the right side of her face smeared with Walker's blood. Chuckler came up on my left side and went to her, leaving me to look for Kris and the kids.

I didn't have to look far.

My stomach dropped to my damn feet as I raced over to where Kris's body was, the sounds of the kids crying barely reaching my ears. Kris was on her side, a pool of blood forming under her body.

No, this could not be happening.

"Kris!" I shouted as the gunfire grew even more distant, grabbing her shoulder and pulling her toward me. Her body just flopped, and for a split second, I thought she was dead.

But then she made a sound and I remembered to breathe. "Kris, babe, you have to stay awake," I said, pulling her against me and pressing my hand hard to the wound at her side. "Look at me, dammit!"

Her eyes fluttered open, the light in them fading fast. "I knew you would come."

"You are damn right I would come," I said, smoothing her hair back from her forehead with my free hand. "You gotta hang on, babe. You can't fucking leave me like this."

She gave me a faint smile before her eyes closed, and I shouted for help, still holding the blood inside of her with my hand.

I couldn't lose her now.

"Shit, man," Ironsides said as he knelt down beside me. "Come on, give her to me. We got a truck waiting."

"She's losing a lot of blood," I said, feeling the tears coursing down my cheeks. "She's not gonna make it."

He pushed my hands away, taking Kris into his own arms. "She'll make it."

I watched helplessly as he carried her out of the house, then looked down at my hands covered in her blood. No, not Kris. They could take me instead, but they couldn't have her.

I wasn't done with her yet, and neither was this world.

Rising on unsteady legs, I saw Leigh and some of the other Bitches tend to Mama Bear's kids, who weren't likely to forget this day for some time.

Hell, I wouldn't be forgetting this day for some time, but I hoped it wasn't because I was about to lose the one woman I loved more than anything in this world.

***

The ride to the hospital was a nightmare. We patched Kris up the best we could, and then hauled ass, pulling up to the ER on two wheels. I didn't even get to see her before they wheeled her to surgery. Some staff waved us off into a waiting room with plastic chairs and little else to go on.

"You have got to stop that," Ironsides muttered as I paced the floor. "You're making me fucking dizzy."

Hell, I had been doing it for the last two hours, finding it difficult to sit still for longer than five minutes. Kris' blood still covered my clothes, my hands scrubbed clean only because they'd made me do it. "When are they gonna let us know something?"

"I don't know," Ironsides said, letting his head fall back against the wall. "But this has to mean something."

I knew what he was trying to say. *They haven't lost her yet.*

The door opened and Mama Bear barreled through, her face streaked with tears. "Where is she?"

"Still in surgery." someone else supplied before I could. About twenty or so people filled the room from both clubs, apparently waiting on me to lose my shit.

Hell, I'd lost it the moment I realized this was it. The moment I'd been desperately trying to keep from happening. I was losing Kris.

"Oh God." Mama Bear came over to me. Before I knew it, she threw her arms around me and sobbed into my chest. "She saved my babies. She risked her life to save them!"

I held onto her, the dull ache in my chest only growing by leaps and bounds. Kris had given her own safety for those kids, and I had never seen anything braver than that. My girl, my woman, the love I would have for the rest of my days, was a fucking angel.

Now if I could only get her in my arms again and know she was going to be alright. I didn't care if she pushed me away, cursed at me, or told me she never wanted to see me again.

I just needed to feel her and make sure she was still my Kris.

"I'm sorry," Mama Bear was saying, pulling back and wiping her eyes at the same time. "I, when they let me out, I knew something bad had happened. I just didn't imagine they would go after my kids and then this would happen."

"None of us did," Siren said, her eyes haunted. "At least Walker is dead."

If he wasn't, I would be hunting him down and shooting him in every place that wouldn't kill him right away. He was the cause of this. Cesar and the Aztecas had gotten away, and I had no doubt we would see them again.

I would be waiting for that day. They actions were a declaration of war against both clubs, and I wasn't going to let this one go.

I knew no one in this room was going to either. "I have to get some air."

No one tried to stop me as I walked out of the waiting room and directly outside, finding a spot against the building I could lean on. My heart was torn to shreds, my entire body numb from the horror of seeing her like that and not being able to do anything about it.

I'd never felt so helpless in my life.

Or scared.

"Hey, you want a light?"

I looked up to see Ironsides standing next to me, his hands in his pockets. "No, I'm good."

"Good. Because I don't have any," he said.

"Why the hell did you ask then?"

"Because," he answered, blowing out a breath. "I thought you needed a moment to think of something else other than the shit going on in there."

I rubbed a hand over my face. "I can't deal with this shit, man. If I lose her…"

"Don't say it," he interrupted me. "She's tough as nails, hell, probably tougher than any of us. She will pull through and be on your ass before you know it."

"I hope so," I said looking up at the sky filled with stars. "I have some making up to do with her." I owed her a shitload of apologies for my actions and an 'I love you' she didn't let me get out when she'd called earlier. I wanted to tell her how I really felt, how she was the very air I breathed, and I didn't want to be separated from her ever again. She could run a dozen clubs and I wouldn't interfere.

Not anymore.

"Come on," Ironsides said, clapping me on the shoulder. "You got your air. People need to see you aren't out here losing your shit."

I blew out a breath this time, sending another dozen prayers to anyone listening up above. "If she doesn't make it, you are gonna have to kill me. Promise me you'll do it."

"Rex," he said.

I shook my head, gripping his shoulder. "No, you don't understand. If she doesn't make it, I'm done for. I want out. I want to be with her and her only."

"Alright," he answered. "Alright. Let's not talk about that unless we have to, okay? Kris is strong. She will make it and you two can have those little fuckers you should have been making years ago. Come on, let's go inside."

I allowed him to push me toward the door, my insides in turmoil. I wasn't just talking. If Kris didn't make it, I didn't want to live.

There would be nothing worth living for.

The moment we got back into the waiting room, the door opened behind us and a man with scrubs walked in, looking as exhausted as I felt.

His gaze widened when he saw the amount of leather-clad people in the room, and he swallowed a few times. "Um, I assume you are all with Ms. Price?"

"Yeah." I stepped forward.

He looked around the room once more before giving a little shrug. "I'm Dr. Robinson, the surgeon on call here tonight. Ms. Price took a bullet to her side, as I'm sure you already know. The bullet cut through her body quite extensively, causing major damage to part of her liver and her spleen. We patched her up the best we could, and with a week or two in the hospital, I think she will make a full recovery."

My knees buckled and I nearly fell to the floor, catching myself just in time. "So, she's awake?"

He shook his head. "No, not yet. We are going to keep her sedated overnight so her body can start the healing process it needs to do. We will let you see her, just as soon as she gets out of recovery."

I turned back and Ironsides was there, grinning

"What did I say?" He said. "I told you she was gonna be alright."

I was starting to believe it.

Chapter 28
Kristina

I fought through the fog in my brain, forcing my eyes to open despite the heaviness trying to keep them closed. The room swam into view and I winced at the sun streaming through the blinds, blinds I didn't recognize.

Why did my mouth feel like one giant cotton ball?

Then, it all came flooding back. The house. Cesar. The kids and Leigh. Oh God, what had happened to them? I remembered running toward them before something bit my side, barely covering them before I lost consciousness.

Was I shot? That had to be what happened.

I turned my head to the side and saw the machines just above it, reading out my vital signs in a steady rhythm.

Well I wasn't dead. This wasn't some weird waiting room before someone decided the fate of my eternal soul.

Looking down, I saw the bulge of a bandage on my left side, the hospital gown concealing just how bad it was. Surprisingly, I didn't feel any pain whatsoever, though I chalked it up to the steady drip of liquid into my IV.

They could keep on doing that.

My vision becoming clearer, I noted a few bouquets of flowers in the room, along with cards lovingly placed on the windowsill as if someone had been reading them to me.

Whoever it had been, I wanted them to appear right now so I could find out where Mama Bear's kids and Leigh were.

And of Brad Walker. I doubted he was still alive given that I had watched his head explode, knowing at that moment it was Rex telling me to run. If Cesar had tried to shoot me, I hadn't known, my mind focused only on getting those kids to safety.

The door opened and Mama Bear walked through, her stride halting as she saw me watching her. "Oh my God, you are awake."

"Apparently," I said, coughing as my voice fought through the cotton.

She hurried to get something off the bedside table, placing a straw in my mouth. "I don't care what they say. A sip of water isn't going to hurt you."

I took a tiny sip, the cool liquid a welcome relief to my dry throat. "Your kids."

"Are shaken up but fine, thanks to you," she finished, placing the cup back on the table. "Tommy doesn't like the dark right now and Violet is having some nightmares, but I am just grateful they are still alive to do so."

"I'm sorry," I said as she turned to face me. "I didn't think."

"Hush," she answered, tears in her eyes. "If you hadn't gone there, I don't know what would have happened. I owe you everything, Kris."

Tears crowded my eyes and I sniffed, glad this conversation hadn't been the other way around. "How did you get out?"

She wiped away her tears, laughing a little. "Well considering the chief of police was found in the company of people known to run with the cartel, the judge didn't see fit to hold me in jail on that ridiculous bail any longer. He lowered it the moment he heard what Walker had done and I was able to spring myself out. Says I have a good chance of looking at probation for this one."

I couldn't be happier. Her kids needed her to stay out of prison. "Was anyone else hurt or killed?"

Mama Bear shook her head. "No, you were the only one besides some Aztecas. Cesar got away, but it's only gonna be a matter of time before he pays for what he did. Chains is going to see to that."

The mention of Rex's name caused my chest to tighten. "Where is he?"

"Oh, he's out there, waiting his turn," she laughed, walking to the door. "I just wanted to let you know I could never repay you for what you did for my kids, Kris. Never. Thank you."

The tears appeared once more, and I lifted my free hand to dash them away. "You're welcome."

She gave me a nod and disappeared through the door, giving me time to prepare myself for Rex and what I was going to say to him.

What would he say to me? Would he tell me this was the very reason he had protected me, so I wouldn't end up in a hospital bed?

Or would he say that being president was far too dangerous, and I would have to choose between the club or him? I hoped not. I didn't know if I could choose either. I loved both of them so much.

He didn't make me wait for long. The moment his face appeared in the doorway, I burst into tears, grateful to see he wasn't injured.

"Hey, hey now," he said, moving to the side of the bed and taking my hand. "It's okay. Don't get yourself upset or they will kick me out again."

"Again?" I asked as he wiped the tears from my cheek.

Rex nodded, his eyes full of emotion. "I may or may not have punched a hole in the wall the night I first saw you in this bed. They threatened to put my ass on trespass notice."

"Rex," I breathed, emotion clogging my throat. "I'm so sorry."

He squeezed my hand gently. "You have nothing to be sorry about, Kris. You saved those kids' lives, Leigh's life. If you hadn't gone there, no telling what would have happened to them." He frowned then, his eyes glancing at my bandaged side. "Though I would rather you not get yourself shot next time."

I chuckled as Rex wiped the remaining tears from my cheeks. "Me neither, though I must be on some good drugs. I can't even feel my side."

"Just wait," he said, linking our hands together. He pulled up a chair next to the bed. "They will probably take the pump away from you tomorrow. Then you will be swearing at all of them."

I squeezed his hand. "Don't leave me."

"I'm not planning to," Rex answered, rubbing his thumb over mine. "Shit, Kris, I'm sorry for what I said that day. You are everything I could never be, for the club, for me, for everyone. I had no right."

I stopped him with a squeeze, forcing him to look at me. "Can we just start over again?" Many things had happened between us, many things I wanted to take back as well, but the past was the past.

I wanted my future, with him.

Rex was quiet for a minute before he drew in a breath, looking at me head on. "Yes, we can, but this time, I'm going to do it right."

"I think we only known how to do it wrong," I said as he untangled our hands. "But I still love you for it."

"Not this time," he said, pressing something into my hand.

I opened it and found a ring there, the diamond winking up at me. "Oh."

"I bought that thing five years ago," he said while I examined the beautiful ring. "I've been holding onto it ever since."

"Rex," I breathed, tears stinging my eyes. "I love you."

He stood and took the ring from my fingers, sliding it where it should have been all these years. "I love you too, Kris. This last week has been hell on me, knowing I could lose you and never get a chance to make you mine, to give you what you deserve." He brought my hand up to his lips, brushing them across my knuckles. "But I would like that chance now."

"Yes," I said, the tears rolling down my cheeks. "A thousand times yes."

He grinned, pressing another kiss to my hand. "This would be where I would have fucked the living daylights out of you, but I think we are gonna have to wait a few weeks."

I pulled him toward me, until our lips were inches from each other. "But that doesn't mean you can't kiss me."

Chapter 29
Rex

I cleared my throat and adjusted my vest in the mirror, wondering why the hell I was so nervous about this. I had waited five long years to marry Kris, but now that the day was finally here, I felt, well, nervous.

"So, you are going to do it," Ironsides grinned, clapping me on the shoulder. "I can't believe it. Of the two of us, I thought I'd tie the knot first."

I snorted. "You've got to get a girlfriend first. Hell, you have to find one who can stand to look at your fucking face."

He shook his head as I adjusted the flower pinned to my vest. "Hey, you never know what might pop up."

I turned, smoothing my beard with my hand. "You got that right. Who would have thought we would be doing this?" After everything Kris and I had gone through, I never would have thought I'd be making her my wife in less than ten minutes.

In two short months, she had gone from laying in a hospital bed nearly dead, to a giddy woman planning her own wedding.

Kris never ceased to fucking amaze me. "You got the ring?"

Ironsides patted his vest pocket. "Right here. Don't worry, dude, I won't lose it. You might want to worry about the maid of honor losing yours. I still can't believe you are actually gonna wear one."

"Me neither," I said, looking at my empty hand. Kris had told me I didn't need to wear a ring, but I wanted to. I wanted to show her I was committed to her and let the rest of the world know I was married.

Mr. President and Madam President. We had taken a lot of ribbing over our engagement from both clubs, but ultimately told them we had no interest in combining the two. They would stay separate and we would do our best to run them as such. "Alright, let's do this shit."

"After you," Ironsides said, moving aside.

I walked out of the room and into the main hall, where we were getting married today. A church didn't feel right, and a recent cold snap had taken out any outdoor options, so we settled on this massive barn instead, where the party would likely go into the wee hours of the morning. Both clubs were present, all dressed in their vests and smiling broadly as I took my place, waiting for the moment Kris would walk down the aisle.

She didn't make me wait long. The doors opened and she walked through, causing me to momentarily forget to breathe when I took in her strapless wedding gown that showed off her sleeves. The gown hugged those curves I knew so well, her hair down her back the way I liked it.

But most of all, it was the damn grin on her face that had me mesmerized, one that I knew matched my own.

"Are you crying?" Ironsides whispered. "Dammit, man, pull yourself together."

I laughed, unable to help it as I wiped my eyes. Who fucking cared if I shed a tear on my wedding day?

After all, I had been waiting on this day for a long, long time.

Kris finally reached my side and reached up, wiping a stray tear from my cheeks, her own eyes shining with tears. "We did it."

"Not yet," I reminded her, taking her hand and wrapping mine around it. "But give us five minutes and we will get it done."

"Are you two ready to do this thing, or what?"

I turned and gave Chuckler a grin, not believing he was going to legally marry us. He hadn't taken the position lightly either, practicing his lines on anyone who would listen for the last week.

"Yeah, we're ready."

"Thank God," he said. "Let's do this thing."

***

Three hours later, the party was in full swing. I drained my beer and grabbed two more as I wandered through the crowd, looking for my wife.

Wife. That had a nice ring to it.

It seemed, though, we spent more time apart than together since tying the knot, every member of our respective clubs wanting to dance with us to firmly welcome us in. I had experienced more ass grabbing than I cared to admit from Kris's club, even dodging a few drunken kisses in the same breath.

But now I wanted a moment alone with my wife.

Finding Mama Bear, I made my way over to her. Both her kids were passed out on the benches, still dressed in their dress clothes. "Have you seen my wife?"

Her cheeks red from the alcohol, her eyes bright, she looked up while thinking. "I think she went back there to change her shoes."

I nodded and walked back to the dressing rooms we had used earlier, pushing open one of the doors before lounging against the doorway. "Mrs. Harper, your husband is looking for you."

Kris grinned from her position against the chair, her face flushed. "Mr. Harper, your wife needs you."

I took in her short dress, the way it rode up her thighs to show off the tops of her lacy stockings. "Damn, he's one lucky man."

"I like to think so," she said with a laugh. "Shut the door Mr. Harper, and come fuck your wife."

I did just that, setting the beers on the table before walking over to her, picking her up by her waist. She squealed as I pressed her against the wall, raining kisses on her neck. "I've been wanting to do just that all night."

"We've got five minutes," she said breathlessly, her hands roaming through my hair. "Before they want us to cut the cake."

"Then I better make it the best damn five minutes of your life," I answered, pressing my cock into her center.

She moaned and I caught it with my mouth, thrusting my tongue inside while my hands slid up her dress, surprised when I met her wet center instead of fabric.

"I took them off," she said against my lip before pulling it into her mouth.

Hell, I loved this woman.

Fumbling with my zipper, I got it open and pulled out my cock, wasting no time burying myself into her warmth.

"Shit, Rex," she said, resting her forehead against my shoulder. "God that feels good."

"Wait until the next minute," I growled, reaching down between us to rub that tight nub I knew waited for my touch. She shuddered around my cock when I found the right spot, applying pressure as Kris gripped my shoulders.

This was going to be fast and furious now, but later on, I planned to kiss every inch of my wife's body. "That's it," I urged, sliding back and forth inside of her. "Let go, Kris."

"Rex," she sobbed. "Yes."

I thrust into her, my fingers working on her clit until she shattered around me, nearly causing me to lose my own shit in the process.

I didn't even need five minutes when she did that.

Grunting, I thrust into her hard, the slapping of our frenzied bodies filling the room until I poured into her with a shout.

"Mr. President," Kris said after a few moments, her voice coming in gasps. "You only took four minutes."

"Shit, Kris," I chuckled, resting my forehead against hers. "I owe you a damn minute then."

She pulled me close, pressing a kiss to my cheek. "I'll let you make it up to me."

Epilogue
Ironsides

Mama Bear enlisted a few Jesters to help her tote her kids out of the barn, leaving me to wonder how the hell she did it being a single parent. She had more balls then the rest of us: handling two kids and be second in command of a bike club at the same time? The woman was a damn saint.

Looking around, I noted both Chains and Widow Maker had made their departure as well, likely going to finish what they started a few hours ago. There was no doubt they had gotten a quickie in right before the cake cutting, the their flushed faces a dead giveaway.

I was happy for both of them, especially my best friend. He had been through some shit over the last five years without Kris by his side, and now that they were a unified pair, I knew they would be a force to be reckoned with.

And I was fine with it. Who cared if they came from two different clubs? I knew them both and they weren't about to jeopardize either club just because they were married now.

I just hoped I could put up with his ass now that he was married and getting some on a regular basis.

Shaking my head, I threw the empty beer bottle in the trash, tucking my hands in my jeans pockets. Most everyone was leaving, on their way to somewhere else so the party could keep going until the sun came up. My head was already spinning from the amount of alcohol I had consumed tonight, and I didn't know how much longer I could last.

A familiar brunette caught my eye and I grinned as I made my way over to her. Maybe if she was going, I could find the strength to keep going.

I would go wherever she was going. "Hey."

Jessie looked up at me and her expression softened, her eyes already bright with alcohol. "Hey."

I stood next to her, so close I could reach out and touch her. I hadn't talked to her all night, watching her from across the room. And more than a few times, our eyes had met. "Good wedding."

She laughed, the sound going straight to my cock. "Yes, it was a good wedding. I think everyone enjoyed it."

"What about you?" I asked, looking over her head at the doors. "Did you enjoy it?"

"Of course," Jessie answered, tugging on her vest. She had just earned the thing a few months ago and was quite proud to be an official member of the Bitches. "They truly love each other. It's the perfect ending for them."

"Or beginning," I said, thinking of how close Rex had come to losing Kris. When he had asked me to kill him if she died, I couldn't even think about it. The terror in his eyes, the pain in his voice, it had all been because he was about to lose Kris. Luckily, she had pulled through and all was good now, but I couldn't shake that moment, when he had thought all hope was lost.

It was why I couldn't get involved like that. I couldn't deal with that kind of helplessness. No, I wouldn't be heading toward a wedding of my own anytime soon, if ever.

Jessie sighed beside me. "Looks like everyone is clearing out."

I nodded, my eyes on hers. "What would you like to do now?"

A smile curved on her lips, telling me what she wanted to do. I knew a lot about her, more than anyone in either club knew.

And no one had suspected us either. We were having fun, two people needing release and finding it at a bar in the middle of the night in the next town over. At the time I hadn't known who she was, and she hadn't known who I was.

Now neither one of us wanted to give up what we had found in each other. "I'm thinking the same."

She ducked her head and I wanted to reach for her, forcing myself to keep my hands in my pockets for now. We had gotten this far without anyone knowing and I wasn't about to blow it because I couldn't wait to touch her. "Your place or mine?"

"Mine," I said, surprising her. I hadn't taken her to my place yet, preferring we meet at a hotel or her place instead.

Maybe it was all this wedding shit, but I was ready to take her there, to let her into my life just a little bit more. It wasn't because I was looking for a relationship, but so that I could show her I trusted her. I wanted to give her what she had been giving me for the last four months. "Follow me."

Jessie looked around before nodding and I started toward the door, feeling the thrill of anticipation flooding my body. Hooking up with Jessie had been unexpected, but since we had started down this path, I couldn't keep my hands off her. The times we did have together seemed to never be long enough.

Walking outside, I noticed a man lurking around the few remaining bikes that stood outside the barn, a man I had seen earlier when I had walked outside for a smoke. He didn't look like a wedding guest. "Do you know that guy?" I asked Jessie in a low voice.

She shook her head, taking a step toward me. "I don't. I've never seen him before."

"Stay here," I told her, seeing no one else around. "I'm gonna find out what he's doing here."

She said something but I was already walking toward him, reaching for my gun I kept against my back, tucked into my waistband. "Hey!"

He looked up and I picked up my pace, daring him to run. I could still chase him down while I was full of alcohol. "Don't even think about running. I just want to talk."

A scream pierced the air and I stopped cold in my tracks, turning around to see Jessie being pushed into a waiting van, a van I hadn't noticed when I walked out.

Shit.

Forgetting about the creeper, I ran toward her, my heart hammering against my chest as the doors shut and the van took off with a screech. I would never catch them at that rate, even if I could find my bike.

Pulling out my gun, I fired a few rounds, but they were already ahead of the bullets, their taillights disappearing into the dark night. For a moment I couldn't think, couldn't breathe.

But then reality came crashing down like a ton of bricks.

Jessie had been taken. She had been kidnapped.

She was gone.

END OF BOOK 1

Because reviews help spread word about my books, please leave a brief review on Amazon or Goodreads if you enjoyed *SAVAGE ANGEL*. Thank you!

OTHER BOOKS BY BROOK WILDER

GHOST RIDERS MC SERIES
BOUGHT
SHACKLED
UNDONE

DEVIL'S MARTYRS MC SERIES
DEVIL'S DEAL
DEVIL'S SEED
DEVIL'S BARGAIN
DEVIL'S PACT
DEVIL'S VOW
DEVIL'S PASSION

ROADBURNERS MC TRILOGY
TAKEN
RUINED
BROKEN

SOUTHERN BIKERS MC SERIES
WRECKED
SHATTERED
DEFILED
PROTECTOR
GUARDIAN
SENTINEL

GRIZZLY MC TRILOGY
TRAPPED
TANGLED
SNARED

Made in the USA
Monee, IL
21 May 2020

31651018R00109